# Sshh-Hop, Skip & Jump

Jimmy Perrin

**Warning:**
This story contains writing of an adult nature
and is only for persons aged 18 or over.

# CONTENTS

DIANE LUCK     TIA KELLY     HILLARY & TEAGAN LUCK

TREVOR LUCK

## DIANE LUCK

Down on her luck Diane is an average housewife that constantly juggles housework, shopping, two teenage daughters and her biggest challenge of all, keeping husband Trevor happy.

Although the 40 year old isn't really a negative person naturally, when things go wrong for her, they do on a massive scale.

With no money ever in the bank and bills mounting up all the time, Diane sometimes forgets to worry about herself and as a result of this, is turning into something of a boring, predictable woman.

## TREVOR LUCK

Laid back Trevor keeps the sanity levels in the house low and with three women around him, he is considered something of a master at it.

It's not because of his laid back nature that he is so successful this way, it's more to do with the fact, he usually leaves all things female to his wife Diane.

Trevor works hard, adores his family, but most of the time will just opt for a quiet life. Saying that, because Diane is starting to turn boring, it is effecting their love life, which is getting him down slightly.

## HILLARY LUCK

Seventeen year old Hillary has a very nice nature, but although she can be loving and supportive, is easily led.

With a male around every corner and a shallow vanity to match, Hillary is turning into something of a slapper to the disapproval of her mother Diane.

Hillary parties hard, drinks like a fish and can also be found hanging with Aunty Tia, who is in-fact Diane's best friend.

## TEAGAN LUCK

Fifteen year old Teagan is the baby of the family and like big sister Hillary, has a very kind heart.

Unfortunately approaching her sixteenth birthday, she's also quickly developing an interest in men like her older sister Hillary.

Teagan is every boys desire at school, yet not because of her looks purely, but because of the slutty uniforms she fashions every day.

Although a virgin, Teagan is planning to lose it at home on her sixteenth in a couple of days, yet parents Diane and Trevor don't know this yet.

## TIA KELLY

Tia went to school with Diane and they've been best friends ever since.

Although Trevor is married to Diane, he often feels he's married to Tia as well, considering the daily visits she makes to their house.

Tia is wild, bubbly and extremely fun.

Unlike Diane, Tia is a self confessed sex addict, with the personality to match.

Whilst Diane constantly reminds her she's a tart and of her age, Tia playfully fights back calling Diane a prude.

# CHAPTER 1
# THE LAND OF PRUDES

It's yet another morning in the Luck family household, as Husband Trevor and wife Diane meet in the kitchen for breakfast. They're always up before their teenage daughters Teagan and Hillary and it's ALWAYS left to mum to scream up the stairs after them every five minutes.

"Teagan, Hillary, times getting on. Let's get a wriggle on, shall we" she calls from the bottom of the staircase, waiting for some sign of life.

"I'm up already, I'm up" grunts Teagan from her bedroom, not sounding pleased that she's been woken.

"Can you make sure Hillary's out of her pit too? Thank you" calls Diane with a big, why do I bother smile on her face.
It's not until Teagan grunts out the information that Hillary isn't in her room, that the forced smile is wiped off her face.

"So where is she then?" mum calls, sounding a little concerned for her seventeen year old daughter.

"Hold on mum, I'll just magically transport myself to wherever she is and ask her" Teagan calls out sarcastically, as she slams the bathroom door closed.

"Thank you" responds Diane, before heading back into the kitchen.
As Trevor rummages through the empty kitchen cupboards for something to eat, Diane watches him from the doorway for a few seconds.

1

"Is there any of that honey cereal stuff left?" he asks, making it clear what he's looking for.

"No sorry, Hillary had the last of that. I will get some more when I'm out shopping today" she answers, before offering him a piece of toast instead.

It's not until she walks over to the bread-bin and finds out it's gone mouldy, that Trevor informs her he will get something to eat on the way to work instead.

"Yeah, you just keep throwing money away and I will magically find more to do the shopping" she responds, in her own non-spiteful sarcastic tone.

Knowing that she doesn't mean to be aggressive in any way, Trevor walks over to her and reassures her everything will be fine.

"Fine? How can you say that?" she asks, with concern in her voice and on her face too.

"We've never got anything in the house, we've hardly any money to replace the missing food and the unpaid bills are building up" she tells him, as he wraps his arms around her.

As she relaxes and takes comfort from his cuddle, Teagan ready for school walks into the room.

"Er, hello... Please tell me that's not what you're wearing to school today" stutters motherly Diane, not impressed at all by Teagan's outfit.

As the blonde schoolgirl stands there looking like she's going out on a hen-night, she turns to Trevor for some support.

"Oh no, don't look at me, I ain't getting involved with girl stuff" he nervously sings, wishing his wife a nice day and giving her a quick kiss.

"You call me when our future son is born and I will handle the boy stuff" he adds heading for the door, giving Teagan a smile, yet a disappointed shake of the head.

"I'M FORTY TREVOR, NOT TWENTY" calls Diane, watching him walk towards the front door.

"Our childbearing days are long behind us, so a little help with OUR daughters would be nice" she adds.

"No problem Honey-bunch. I will start helping tomorrow" he responds with a smile, before shutting the door behind him.

Left down to her as usual, Diane knows she must now tackle the Teagan situation herself this morning, so turns back to her daughter. She looks

2

her up and down, without the disappointed look her father gave her, then tries to talk some sense into her, whilst feeding her compliments.

"Mum, I know what you're trying to do and you really should stop" Teagan tells her, insisting she isn't going to get changed.

"Oh but Sweetie, I just wish you could see what me and your father can see in you" responds Diane, still opting for the softly, softly approach.

"You are so beautiful and don't need to show off so much, er?... Flesh in order to get boys to notice you. You get enough of that sort of attention already" she adds, hoping she's making a breakthrough of some kind.

"Mum, the reason I get so much attention, is because I dress like this" Teagan explains, claiming that's exactly the way she likes it.
With neither of them willing to back down and in a conversation they aren't having for the first time, Diane turns to the more demanding motherly approach and insists she isn't leaving the house looking like that.

"And who's going to stop me?" huffs Teagan, as the relaxed mood threatens to kick off.

"You are FIFTEEN years old young lady, there's no way I am letting you out of MY house looking like that" snaps Diane.

"Sixteen next week mum, sixteen next week" responds Teagan heading for the door.

"And if you don't let me be my own person by then, you won't see me anymore, just like Hillary" she adds, hitching up her already short skirt in front of the hallway mirror, before telling her mum she loves her and to stop being so prudish, as she opens the front door.

"Oh okay then Sweetie, I will. Have a nice day, love you" calls Diane, unsure of how to react to the prudish comment that is getting more and more frequent these days.
Just as Teagan steps out of the door, Diane's best friend Tia is on the other side, waiting to come in.

"Looking damn sexy, Teagan baby" chirps Tia, instantly giving the naughty daughter her own seal of approval.

"Thank you AUNTY Tia" Teagan replies, turning back to her mother inside and poking her tongue out cheekily.
As if it's not another conversation Diane finds herself frequently in the

middle of, she then frowns at her best friend walking in and asks her not to encourage her daughter.

"You've got a sexy young daughter looking as good as she does and you mummy, don't want to tell her so?" questions Tia, walking into the kitchen.

"I have a FIFTEEN year old daughter looking like that and NO I don't want her to go out looking like that" answers Diane, making her valid motherly point.

It's not until the kettle is switched on and Tia tells Diane to take a chill-pill, that the mood starts to ease a little, as Tia pays Diane her usual compliment.

"It's not your daughters fault she looks as hot as her mum" she says.

"Well... Before she stopped making an effort and decided baggy jumpers were her thing" she adds.

"Excuse me? What's wrong with my jumpers? And who said I stopped making an effort?" responds Diane, a little insulted by her friends playful comment.

"It's okay for you dressed in that skirt, wearing long sexy boots and throwing your chest out at every man, but I'm a responsible mother and a wife" she adds.

"And that's why I am a MILF and you're not" chirps Tia, deciding now is the best time to get a big head and gloat about herself.

"Milf? Milf?" giggles Diane.

"Yeah you know, MILF... Mother I'd like to...."

"Yes, yes Tia, I know what it means, thank you" grunts Diane, cutting her friend off mid-sentence, so she doesn't crude up their conversation.

"But you're forgetting one vital ingredient, don't you think?" she asks.

"Oh yeah and what's that exactly?" moans Tia checking herself out, in-case she didn't oversize or flaunt anything incorrectly on the way over this morning.

"You're not a bloody mother, are you?" answers Diane, using strong enough language to consider it bad language in her tame vocabulary.

As the debate starts up again and the two friends both aged forty, playfully argue like a couple of school girls, Tia continues to make her point about Diane not making the effort anymore and Diane continues to call her friend a tart.

"My, my, my... We are Miss Grumpy-Knickers this morning, aren't we?" laughs Tia, asking her best friend what's really on her mind.

Although Diane tells Tia absolutely everything and vice-versa in their solid friendship, Diane doesn't want to talk about her money problems again. Especially as the last time was exactly two weeks ago today and EVERY two weeks on this day before that.

"It's money again, isn't it?" Diane guesses, knowing her friend far too well.

"No, it's not money actually" answers Diane, not wanting her friend to be correct about anything right now.

"Well it's either that, or Miss Grumpy-Knickers isn't getting any" responds Tia.

"Ah... Didn't Trevy-Wevey stick his thicky-dickey somewhere special last night?" she asks, mocking her friend and her prudish ways.

"Tia stop it... That's disgusting" quivers Diane, adamant she's not having this rude conversation.

"Didn't his thicky-dickey, satisfy your clitty?" sings Tia.

"Didn't mumsey-wumsey, get it up the bumsey last night?" she continues to sing, pushing and pushing her friends blushes to the limit.

"THAT'S ENOUGH !!" growls embarrassed Diane, still giggling a little bit herself.

"There's nothing wrong with mine or Trevor's sex life, I will have you know" she adds.

"You... Dirty... Slut" Tia huffs very slowly.

"So you DID let him shag you up the bumsey-wumsey last night" she adds, sounding a little jealous and showing she wants all the details.

"Eww, you are gross Tia, gross" sings Diane, unable to keep up with her vulgar chat any more, insisting she herself doesn't do weird stuff in the bedroom, like someone she doesn't want to mention right in front of her.

With that Tia bursts out laughing...

"Don't do weird stuff? Don't do weird stuff?" she laughs.

"Says the woman that licked my fanny when we were eighteen years old" she adds.

Knowing it was coming, Diane as she usually does, claims the event in question ONLY happened once, will NEVER happen again and she's not bi-sexual like the tart sitting opposite her.

"Anyone listening to you now, would think you regret it" sighs Tia, trying to sound upset by the outburst.

"We've discussed this before Tia... SOOOO many times" explains Diane.

"I will never regret it, BUT... It's just not me, I don't do women" she adds, explaining she grew-up years ago, whereas Tia never did.

"Fair enough, point taken" says beaten Tia, knowing the conversation is finally coming to an end.

"Thank you... Now please, NEVER speak of it again" demands Diane, wiping the nervous sweat from her brow.

As Tia agrees never to mention it again, like she has promised so many times before, she heads through into the living room, then pops her head back round the door frame...

"F.Y.I... It never came out of my mouth that day. It came out of my fanny and into yours" she giggles, as Diane gives chase to kick her butt playfully.


Once the two grown women have had their morning of usual merriment, things start to get on top of Diane again when her friend has left an hour later. She sits down at the kitchen table, looks around the room, then tries to prioritise what the house needs most from the shop on the tiny budget she has. In a drawn-up shopping list that would take a normal person with money minutes to write, Diane's mini list takes just over half an hour, as she adds things to it, then scribbles them out because they are simply too expensive.

With her shopping list almost complete, Diane is then shocked when Tia bounces back through the front door.

"Back so soon Tia? Didn't you realise it wasn't morning again yet?" Diane sarcastically chirps, wanting to dig at her friend instantly, yet being secretly pleased to see her again.

Tia walks into the kitchen and hands over a pair of really tight jeans.

"What's this?" asks confused looking Diane.

"If I can lend you something of mine, to get you back to who you once were, or even a millimetre closer, then I will be happy" explains Tia, claiming that's step one of her friends recovery from the land of prudes complete.

Grateful for her friends offer, yet slightly confused as in to what it's actually going to do for her, Diane accepts the gift as the phone rings. As she walks across the kitchen to answer it and Tia follows her, insisting the jeans must be put on now; Diane faces a tussle with the phone cord and her friend at her waist, trying to unbutton the jeans she already has on.

"Hello" she says answering the phone.

"Get off me, I will do it in a minute" she adds, talking to Tia at her knees at the same time.

It's not until a BIG "Oh no" comes out of Diane's mouth, that Tia stops and stands up to find out what's wrong.

Whilst Diane finishes her conversation and tells the person on the other end of the phone she will be there as soon as she can, Tia wants to know what's going on.

"That was the school, it's Teagan" sighs Diane.

"What is it?" giggles Tia, knowing it can't be that bad.

"What, did she forget to put some knickers on underneath her belt this morning?" she asks, trying to lighten the fading mood.

Diane quickly explains that the school urgently need to see her in order to discuss her daughter's behaviour.

"What's she done, refused to give the Maths teacher head or something?" asks Tia, still making light of it all.

"NO !!" grunts Diane, asking her friend to stop messing around.

"Okay then, the Science teacher?" responds Tia.

Once Tia has stopped fooling around, Diane asks her to accompany her to the school for some moral support.

"Er, yeah, er... Sorry, I can't" Tia responds at a stutter, yet quite bluntly.

"I think you've already pointed out this morning that I ain't no MILF, which means I DON'T do parenting or schools whatsoever" she adds.

Diane knows that her friend isn't going to budge on the subject, so instead asks her if she can take her shopping list and do that for her instead.

"Oh babes, although there's nothing more I want to do than help you, I was only popping in to drop off these jeans, before going to the er, er?... To get waxed" Tia explains, lying through her teeth of course.

"Tia, you have no hair to wax" sighs Diane.

"OH YEAH and how would you know that Miss Prude Pants? Miss, I

7

don't do or look at girls anymore?" barks playful Tia.

"Because when we go swimming once a week Tia, you constantly show me your thingy, then ask me if I am a lesbian again" answers Diane, as if she really needed to answer the question in the first place.
Before Diane can get a response or another playful jib out of her friend, Tia is making her way towards the front door, wishing her luck at the school.

"OH... You've got to go now, have you? THANKS FOR ALL YOUR HELP THEN" calls Diane from the kitchen, as she hears the front door close.

"I bet if I said I needed help out of these jeans, you wouldn't be leaving so quickly" she grumbles to herself, dreading the school and supermarket trips alone now.

"Why? Do you need help with them?" asks Tia, magically appearing from behind the wall, as Diane jumps out of her skin.

"No I don't, thanks" gasps the shocked mum, clutching at her chest.

"O-Kay then, I will see you later" sings Tia, walking out of the front door, this time for real.


Half an hour later Diane finds herself sitting in the headmaster's office at the school, waiting for a teacher to come and talk to her. Feeling like a little girl in trouble herself, she looks around the room and instantly remembers what it's like to be back there. Soon enough a jobs-worth teacher walks into the room and cuts to the chase. He tells Diane that her daughter doesn't try at school, is rude when asked something and dresses far too inappropriately.

"Wow, is that all? I thought you were going to expel her or something" responds Diane, using comedy as a defence mechanism.

"We will have no choice but to expel her, if she doesn't buck up her ideas Mrs Luck" groans the teacher, not seeing the funny side at all.
With that the comedy defence mechanism takes over completely and Diane rudely, but unintentionally starts giggling.

"Sorry, it's just you said Buck and Luck in the same sentence" Diane sniggers, telling herself off for laughing, then trying desperately to stop herself.
With a tear in her eye, finally the giggling has stopped, but only when the teacher insults her and claims parents should control their children

better at home, and act like an adult themselves in front of them.

"Excuse me, but I am a good mother, thank you very much" grunts Diane, feeling the need to defend herself properly now.

"I'm sure you are Mrs Luck, but your daughters behaviour I'm afraid, doesn't show this" says the pompous teacher, putting her down yet again.

As Diane sits there nervously getting attacked for being the GOOD mother she is, she clutches onto her shopping list as tightly as she can and hopes the ground will swallow her up.

"There's no place like home, there's no place like home" she whispers to herself, clicking her heels together, hoping the Wizard of Oz thing really does work.

**STRANGELY, NOTHING HAPPENS !!**

She is warned again by the horrid teacher to improve her daughter's outlook on life, then shown the door herself. She politely thanks the teacher for his time, then steps into the corridor feeling beaten, abused and dejected. As she stands there wanting to cry and feeling a little wobbly on her feet, she scrunches up her shopping list and starts to feel angry.

"Thank you very much, ruby slippers" she grumbles to herself, looking down at her feet.

"I might as well have hopped, skipped and jumped, for all the use you were" she adds, hopping, skipping and jumping like a crazy woman down the corridor.

Just then as she lands her huge skip, a light headedness echoes out around her already wobbly body and she feels like she's about to pass out. As the corridor begins to spin and the classroom doors move around on their own, Diane closes her eyes tightly, falls against the wall and hopes her dizzy spell will pass.

"Thank you very much, please come again" says a random voice.

Confused Diane still spinning, opens her eyes, then if she wasn't confused enough already, finds herself standing in the supermarket at the check-out.

"Thank you very much, please come again" says the cashier, handing her a bag of shopping.

# CHAPTER 2
## HOP, SKIP & JUMP

Startled Diane spins on the spot for a few seconds longer, trying to remember how she got to the supermarket from the school, then tries even harder to remember doing the shopping she's apparently just finished.

"Thank you very much, please come again" says the cashier for a third time, waiting for Diane to pick up her bag and move away from the checkout, so he can serve the next customer.

"Er, yeah, er, okay... Thank you?" she stutters, finally understanding what the cashier is trying to say, noticing the queue of people behind her getting impatient and giving her funny looks.

She takes the bag, then without checking through the items inside, walks towards the exit of the supermarket, as she then realises she didn't do the shopping, she can't have...

"Please tell me I ain't going mad, please tell me I ain't going mad" she mumbles to herself out loud, ironically making her look like a mad person to passers-by.

She gets outside the shop and once again tries hard to remember entering the building in the first place, but can't. She then stops beside the ATM and finally looks through the bag.

"Honey cereal, eggs and milk" she says to herself, noticing everything on her shopping list is in the bag.

Finally searching for the proof needed, she pulls out her purse and decides to check the money situation inside.

"Oh dear..." she then grumbles in shock, falling against the wall, as she notices the money for the shopping still in there.

"I don't remember getting here from the school or doing the shopping and now it seems I haven't paid for any of it either" she say to herself, claiming she is actually going mad.

Now feeling like a shoplifter, she stands there juggling with her own emotions. On one hand, it seems she's been handed a bag of shopping without paying, which means she has a little spare cash for other things now. On the other hand, it's wrong and dishonest and she won't be able to sleep tonight if she doesn't get to the bottom of it. Before she can think any further, honest Diane finds herself strolling back into the shop and towards the cashier.

"Er, excuse me" she uncomfortably utters, trying to get his attention, as he sits there serving his next customer.

"Did you give me a receipt for my shopping, because I can't find it?" she questions.

As she stands there and opens her purse ready to pay for the obvious mistake, she is then knocked sideways once more, when he confirms the receipt is in the bottom of her bag and he knows this because he watched her put it there.

"Oh of course I did, silly me" she responds, with a baffled looking smile on her face.

"I'd forget my own head, if I didn't screw it on every morning" she adds, trying to make light of the situation, yet feeling that a VERY stiff drink is needed right now.

Once back outside the shop, on a mission she rummages through the bag and finally pulls out the receipt.

"Okay, so I did pay for the shopping, that's good" she tells herself looking at the piece of paper.

"But why is the shopping money still in my purse then?" she questions, looking completely baffled once again.

"Maybe I had more money than I thought I did? Yeah that's it, that's the only explanation for it" she continues to mumble, hoping this logical reason is the reason, although she knows it's not really the reason for the mystical happenings.

Half an hour later, shopping bag firmly in hand, Diane walks into her house, remembering every single step she made on the way home.

"See, I remember walking to the school. I remember walking home, so why don't I remember going to the shop?" she questions herself at her front door.

"Maybe it was the stress of that not so nice teacher" she adds, making this now her logical explanation for the bizarre shopping trip, as she enters her house and into the kitchen.

"Hello mum, fancy a coffee?" asks seventeen year old Hillary, back from wherever she's been, freshly out of the shower, wrapped in a towel.

"Oh Hi Sweetie, Yes please, extra strong" responds Diane, putting her mystery bag of shopping on the table, then taking a seat.

"Mum, were you talking to yourself when you walked in?" asks Hillary, as she makes the coffee.

"No, why would you ask that? Was I? Why, do I always talk to myself then?" responds confused Diane sitting at the table, panicking with her three question response.

Before Diane can lose her mind completely, she notices that Hillary's home from wherever she's been all night, then notices that her daughter is uncharacteristically making her a cup of coffee.

"So Sweetie, where were you last night?" questions Diane, finally finding her sanity and becoming a concerned mother once more, expecting a brutal telling off for asking such an inquisitive question.

"Oh yeah right, sorry... I should have called" Hillary answers again in an uncharacteristic adult fashion, claiming she stayed over at Melina's house to watch a film.

As if Diane needed shocking any more, she just can't get her head around why her usually irate daughter is being so nice to her.

"What do you want Hillary?" Diane finally asks, realising what it's all about, yet understanding nothing really.

"Nothing mum, I don't want anything" answers her daughter, with a guilty smile that says otherwise.

"I will ask you once more Hillary, then whatever it is you want, you won't get" responds Diane, putting her gentle motherly foot down.

13

"Well now you mention it, mum..." grins Hillary, handing her the cup of coffee.

"I've seen these boots I really like" she adds, confessing all.

As Diane takes her shopping list notepad from the table and starts to take details of the boots in question, Hillary is a little overwhelmed at just how easy it is.

"What you mean I can have them? No questions? No excuses about not having any money?" she stutters, asking three questions in concession herself now.

Knowing there's strangely enough money in her purse this morning and realising that her daughters never get treated to anything really, Diane smiles and continues to write the details down. Just as her pen touches the notepad, Tia walks back into the house for a third time today.

"Hello Slut-face" she says to Hillary, playfully.

"Hello Aunty Whore-bag" answers Hillary, giggling at their usual friendly banter.

"Not pregnant yet then? Or is the towel something you've fashioned up as a make-shift maternity dress?" Tia asks, showing the youngster no-one does wit better than she does.

With that Diane steps in and demands they stop talking to each-other like this.

"What? Dirty little Hillary knows I'm only playing" responds Tia, knowing all too well that Diane would say something eventually.

"Yeah well, my daughter isn't like that, thank you very much" Diane gently barks.

"Yeah and I've got a pair of knickers on underneath this skirt today" Tia responds sarcastically, hitching up the backside of the said skirt, giving her friend a quick flash of cheek, then asking at a whisper if she's a lesbian yet.

As Diane blushes, then tells her to shut up without words, the conversation runs dry.

"Pub?" asks Tia, looking at Hillary.

"Sure" giggles Hillary, happy that she's getting her new boots.

"Seventeen !!" snaps Diane from the table, feeling the need to remind her friend of her daughters' age.

"Yes, yes Diane Grumpy-Knickers... Seventeen, meaning old enough to walk into a pub" sings Tia.

"Yeah but not old enough to drink" responds Diane.

As Hillary informs Tia that she's just going upstairs to get dressed, Tia agrees with her friend that only soft drinks will be consumed at the pub, with a little secret wink in Hillary's direction.

Whilst Tia waits for Hillary to get dressed or undressed as the finished article may turn out, Diane then remembers that her friend was going to get waxed earlier, so questions her.

"Oh yeah, I was, wasn't I" responds Tia, mumbling something about there being a reason she wasn't supposed to turn up at the house again today.

"Well?... I thought the reason you couldn't come shopping or to the school with me, is because of this wax you so desperately needed?" asks Diane, waiting to catch her friend out.

"Oh yeah, well in the end I, er... I decided I..."

"You were NEVER going to get waxed, were you Tia?" Diane huffs, interrupting her friends bumbling.

"No" sighs Tia, lowering her head in shame.

"So what did you really have to do then?" asks Diane, waiting for the next lie or excuse.

"Yeah, what it was, er... I went to the, er..." stutters lost Tia, before confessing all in a rapid outburst...

"I didn't want to come out boring food shopping with you and couldn't be bothered to sit in a shitty school, listening to a shitty teacher moan about nothing" she explains, blurting out the whole truth finally, before asking Diane if she's happy now.

With nothing else to say on the matter, Diane gives her a big smile and although doesn't say it, tells her friend she could have just been honest in the first place.

"I'm really sorry Diane, I just couldn't..."

"It's okay Tia, I understand" Diane giggles, as Tia's porkies turn into complete guilt.

"I just didn't want to, you know, sit at school or..."

"Seriously Tia, it's okay, I understand" Diane reassures her friend again.

"I mean, I would rather put my beloved dildo down and masturbate with a pineapple anally, than sit listening to a teacher talk crap" Tia explains.

15

Before Tia can erupt any more filthy reasons, Hillary comes back downstairs in a shorter skirt than Tia's this morning, a cropped-top looking more like a bra and ironically what looks to be newish boots on her feet.

"Looking damn hot, Hillary baby" sings Aunty Tia, giving her a wolf whistle.

"Mum?" asks Hillary, doing a little twirl in front of them both.

"You look really nice Sweetie, really nice" Diane answers with a smile, yet the smile as usual giving off a different answer altogether.
With that forty year old Tia and seventeen year old Hillary depart for the pub, leaving Diane to sit at the table, thinking about her crazy shopping trip again and ready to order Hillary's so desperately not needed boots.

"Okay, boots, order the boots" she mumbles, telling herself not to think about the shopping trip any more, as she opens her laptop.

"MM-mm, I wonder..." she then asks herself, remembering something that happened at the school before she magically appeared in the supermarket, as the shopping page loads in front of her on the screen.
She stands up with an idea, rips the shopping list consisting of a pair of boots from the notepad, then scrunches it up. She then hops, waits... Skips, waits... And finally jumps in her kitchen.

"Oh my god, not again" she panics, as the room starts to spin, her vision goes blurry and the toaster does a little dance of its own on the counter.

"Surely not... This can't be happening" she stutters, trying to feel for the chair behind her, expecting any second to come round at the check-out of the online store, talking to a cashier.
She closes her eyes tightly and waits for it to happen again...

# CHAPTER 3
## SPECIAL DELIVERY

"Thank you very much, please come again" she mumbles over and over again to herself, with her eyes tightly closed.

**NOTHING !!**

"Thank you very much, please come again" she mumbles once more.

**NOTHING AGAIN !!**

As her head stops spinning a few minutes later and she tempts to open her eyes, she stops mumbling to herself, just in-case her own voice is drowning out the cashier she wants to hear.

**NOTHING !!**

Finally after another sixty seconds, she opens her eyes...

A quick sense of relief shudders through her body, as the magic she was expecting didn't actually happen. Then quicker than a flash, disappointment kicks in as she realises her dream come true money saving idea, didn't work. Diane quickly reassures herself she isn't going mad, then sits down to drink her now warm coffee.

"Wow, it would have been so nice if it was real" she says to herself, before realising she's talking to herself again, so stands up, shakes it off and declares out loud she's going for a shower.

"Who are you telling Diane? Stop bloody talking to yourself" she says, ironically still talking to herself, as she heads for the bathroom.

Half an hour later whilst enjoying the steam from the shower, lathering herself up with soap and bubbles, her tiny piece of sanity is interrupted by a knock at the front door...

"Why do you do this Tia? Why do you walk in most of the time, then knock when it's inconvenient?" she mumbles to herself, knowing it can only be one person, as she wraps a towel around her wet body.

She races down the staircase, then shock hits her again for the fourth time today, as there stands a delivery guy...

"Er... Yes, er... Can I help you?" she stutters nervously, realising straight away that she's naked underneath her towel and there's a random young man standing in front of her.

"Delivery?" the man confusingly questions, as if the uniform and package in his hand aren't obvious answer enough.

"Yeah, but.. I... I'm not expecting anything" she stutters, getting the knickers she isn't wearing in a right twist.

"You are Mrs Luck, yeah? This is 26 Foundamore Road, right?" he asks.

"Er... Yeah, that's right" she continues to nervously stutter, trying to pull her towel more tightly around her body, yet ironically flashing more flesh than she should be in the process.

"Then I DO have a delivery for you" responds the man handing her a box, trying desperately to steer his eyes away from her flashing cleavage.

Diane takes the box, then before signing for it, opens it, as he just stands and waits.

"Oh Shi...ugar" she gargles, as her legs buckle and she collapses into his arms...

The shock of the new boots inside the box hits Diane like a lightning bolt and as the delivery guy catches her and gently lowers her down towards the floor, Tia returns from the pub...

"Oh yeah, good one Diane. I've played the damsel in a wet towel distress fantasy out before too" she chirps, stepping over her passed-out friend and the delivery guy, convinced her dirty prudish friend has been caught out.

"Like mother like daughter eh..." she adds, informing unconscious Diane, that her dirty daughter has pretty much done the same thing in the pub and gone off with a random guy too.

As the concerned delivery guy continues to try and bring Diane round, whilst insisting she isn't play-acting, suspicious Tia isn't buying it.

"She passed out, did she? Just happened to collapse in your arms, wrapped in a towel, did she?" Tia responds in a high pitched, unconcerned tone.

"Then why don't you help her young man and carry her up to the bedroom... You know, to make her feel more comfortable" she suggests, playing along with Diane's attempt at seduction, although it isn't really a seduction attempt.

Feeling the older woman knows best, the delivery guy wraps his arms around poor Diane and lifts her up.

"That's it, carry her up to the bedroom and lay her gently on her bed... Good boy" sings Tia, claiming Diane is playing her part really well.

"Watch your hand doesn't slip up her towel on the way" she adds, playing out her own vision of a porn scene, shadowing them up the staircase.

Tia follows the delivery guy and dying duck Diane up to the bedroom, where he continues to follow the instructions given. He lays her on the bed, then waits for his next command, as he looks down at the unconscious woman in her towel.

"Now slowly undo the towel top end first and take it off" orders Tia, playing the part of a pornographic director now, as she gets into her role fully.

"Christ Diane... You could have picked up your dirty knickers, before deciding to seduce a man into your bedroom" she adds breaking character, picking up Diane's underwear from her bedroom floor, then flicking them to safety over in the corner.

As Tia slips straight back into character, she is then startled herself, when she notices the delivery guy not following through with her next demand.

"Come on young man, get that towel off her. What are you waiting for?" she huffs at him, showing her instant disappointment.

"Is this right? I mean, should I be doing... I only came to deliver a package" he stutters nervously, finally realising himself what he's in the middle of.

"Package? Package? Then deliver your package... Give her your BIG,

ENORMOUS package" sings Tia, egging him on.

He nervously realises he isn't going to escape the room alive, if he doesn't deliver what he's not there to deliver, so looks at Diane again and places his hand on the top of the towel.

"MM-mm, Tre...vor" grumbles Diane, eyes closed in wonderland.

"ER... YEAH... DIANE... Not exactly appropriate to mention your husband's name at a time like this" sighs Tia.

"Well, unless you're playing out the cheating wife seduction porno, in which case, go for it girl... YOU GO FOR IT" she adds, getting more and more excited.

With the noise her friend is making and the touch of the delivery guy's hand, Diane opens her eyes slowly, then widely as she starts to scream the house down...

"WHAT? Er... Help... WHY? TIA? HOW?" she panics, sitting up rapidly, then securing the towel once again.

"Sorry young man, I think your time here is done" sighs Tia, watching her friend freak out, then ordering him to leave, because it looks like Diane has changed her mind.

"NEXT TIME YOU FIND YOURSELF IN THIS SITUATION, GET YOUR DICK OUT FASTER" she calls out, watching him nervously leaping down the staircase.

Tia looks at her friend on the bed and simply shakes her head in disappointment.

"How did I?... What happened? Who was that?" stutters Diane, trying to find her bearings after coming round again.

"Diane, Diane, Diane... If you're going to play out the seduction in a towel routine, make sure you want to do it first" sighs Tia, sitting down on the edge of the bed with her friend, claiming the poor young man is probably going to masturbate himself to death now.

"How?... I... What, er..." Diane continues to stutter.

"Poor, poor boy... All stiff and hard, expecting to..." says Tia, before stopping herself mid-sentence, leaping off the bed and giving chase down the stairs.

A few minutes later as a more composed Diane still in her towel walks downstairs, Tia comes bouncing back through the front door...

"Gone, bloody gone, hasn't he?" Tia huffs, sounding really disappointed.

"Little shit saw me coming, locked his doors and drove away" she adds, blaming Diane's prudish behaviour.

Once all the confusion, disappointment and weird commotions have finished, the two women sit in the kitchen discussing the subject in hand. Diane explains that it was never a seduction attempt and she simply passed out in shock.

"Oh yeah, shock of what exactly?" suspicious Tia questions, not believing a word of it.

"Shock that his trouser snake was really big? Or shock that your prudish self could ever go through with something like that?" she asks, adamant Diane is lying.

Knowing that she can't tell the truth about her secret shopping trick, Diane needs to think fast, so comes up with an excuse about the delivery time.

"Oh don't tell me... It's the first time you've ever used a 24hour delivery service?" huffs Tia, still not buying it.

"Why don't you just admit it? You wanted to shag a younger man, did the towel routine thing, really convincingly by the way, then bottled it at the last minute" she adds, giving her very own theory on the event.

"No, it's nothing like that Tia, really... This delivery is REALLY fast" Diane insists, trying desperately to convince her friend she wouldn't cheat on Trevor and she should know that.

"Come on then. How fast was this delivery?" asks Tia, still not buying it.

"Thirty minutes" answers Diane, knowing that's the truth after all.

"Thirty minutes? OH NO..." sighs disappointed Tia again, stopping mid-sentence again.

"We could have had a bloody threesome with him, then I could have stuck my fanny in your face again" she adds, pointing out quickly what the "Oh no" was for.

Unhappy that her friend doesn't believe her, Diane decides there's only one thing for it and that is to prove it. She tells Tia to pick a perfume from the online store on the laptop in front of them, then assures her it will turn up within thirty minutes.

"Thirty minutes? A perfume? From this site?" questions Tia, doubting her every word.

"Okay then Miss I didn't want to shag the young delivery guy... Let's see this work" she adds, knowing Diane will have to tell the truth when it doesn't show up.

Tia quickly searches for a perfume, then picks one.

"Are you sure that's the one you want? It's only £9.99" questions confused looking Diane, claiming tight Tia doesn't have to pay for it and that she will.

"Oh you're buying it, are you Grumpy Knickers? Okay then..." responds Tia, looking back at the screen, then quickly picking out a £4.99 bottle.

"Money isn't an option Tia... ANY perfume you like" says Diane, wanting her to try one more time.

"Okay this one... This one I will NEVER be able to afford at £58 a bottle, which I know ISN'T going to turn up within thirty minutes anyway or EVER for that matter" she giggles, finding the whole thing laughable and such a waste of time.

As Diane grabs her magical notepad from the kitchen table and writes down the name of the perfume, she tells Tia to stick the kettle on, whilst she quickly does something in the other room.

"Now if your perfume does turn up within half an hour, you're going to go home and NEVER mention the delivery guy incident again" says Diane.

"Ah see, now it's an IF it turns up" Tia chirps, searching for the catch.

"Okay then... WHEN it turns up, you are to NEVER mention this again" Diane responds, rephrasing her statement for her suspicious friend.

Once Tia has agreed and walks towards the kettle, Diane tears the piece of paper out of the notepad, scrunches it up and heads through into the living room alone.

"Don't make me regret this notepad... Don't let me down right now" she nervously sings to herself, checking that Tia isn't around, then doing her hop, skip and jump thing...

Instantly the lightheadedness hits her hard, but prepared for it now, she deals with it much better. She falls against the door so Tia can't walk in, closes her eyes, then makes some groaning noises instead.

"Is everything okay in there Miss Seduction in a towel?" calls Tia from outside the room.

"I don't mean to mention it, but you should be ordering my make-believe perfume right now and not flicking your bean, fantasising about the delivery guy" she adds.

Two minutes later, looking as though she HAS just masturbated, Diane emerges from the room, claiming her friends perfume is on its way.

"Enjoy that did you? Better than the real thing, was it?" asks Tia, handing her friend a cup of coffee, claiming she's going mad or is sexually deprived.

As the two friends sit at the table in silence for a while, waiting for this non-existent, magical delivery to turn up, Tia's patience begins to wear thin...

"It's not coming, is it?" she asks Diane.

"You were playing out seduction in a towel, weren't you?" she asks, demanding her friend stop playing games.

"It WILL be here Tia" responds Diane, pleading with her friend to be more patient.

"Oh yeah, when?" asks Tia, doubting her friend more and more by the second.

"In exactly twenty-seven minutes... Considering it was only three minutes ago I ordered the thing" answers Diane.


After a full twenty-nine minutes of Tia begging Diane to stop boring her to death with this crazy delivery idea, yet another cup of coffee and Diane managing to get dressed again, the doorbell rings...

"If this is my perfume, I will chop off my clitoris and lick it myself" gasps Tia, still not convinced it's a delivery at all.

Diane feeling confident about what's going to happen next, strolls to the door with a huge smirk on her face, as a suspicious Tia follows... As the door opens and a different delivery guy stands there, Tia herself threatens to go all wobbly at the knees and falls against the wall.

"You okay there Tia? Looks as though you are about to seduce someone" giggles Diane, signing for the delivery and opening the box.

As Tia refuses to pass-out and give Diane the last laugh, she stands up, takes the expensive bottle of perfume and pushes past the delivery guy on the doorstep.

"TIA, MY BEDROOMS THIS WAY IF YOU WANT TO PASS OUT" calls

Diane from her doorstep, thanking the confused delivery guy, then watching her friend gallop off down the road.

"FORGET SEDUCTION BABES" Tia calls back.

"ONCE THE BOYS DOWN THE PUB GET A WHIFF OF THIS AROUND MY KNICKERS, I WILL BE IN THE MIDDLE OF A BLOODY GANGBANG" she adds, disappearing out of sight.

Once Tia has gone for the last time today and the latest delivery guy has been waved off, Diane picks her daughters new boots off the floor and heads into the kitchen. She sits down at the table and looks at her magical notepad.

"I never have to pay for anything ever again" she gasps to herself.

"No more money worries EVER" she adds, letting her confused, lost smile shine.

# CHAPTER 4
# DOCTOR SPOCK

Once again it's yet another morning in the Luck family household, yet this morning as Trevor and wife Diane meet in the kitchen, she secretly knows something is different. As usual the parents are up before daughters Teagan and Hillary, then once again it's up to Diane to scream them out of their beds.

"Teagan, Hillary, times getting on. Let's get a wriggle on, shall we" she calls at the bottom of the staircase, having no time this morning to wait for signs of life.

Whilst both teenagers drag themselves out of bed and Diane in the kitchen helps herself to a bowl of Trevor's Honey cereal, they know the girls are up as they start fighting to get into the bathroom first. Trevor looks over at Diane, as if he already knows what happens next, but for some reason this morning she doesn't scream out again, she just continues to eat her cereal with a smile fixated on her face.

"You okay this morning Darling?" asks Trevor, a little shocked.

"Yeah, why?" she chirps, still munching away.

"You not going to deal with those two upstairs?" he asks, hearing the crashing and banging from where he's sitting.

"Are you going to deal with it Sweetie? No? Then neither am I?" she answers, beaming from ear to ear, as Trevor's face drops and he thinks he's woken up in the wrong house.

As Trevor sits there trying to figure out what's got into his wife this morning, things aren't helped much when youngest daughter Teagan comes downstairs ready for school. Trevor looks at his daughter in her short denim skirt and baggy torn shirt, he immediately looks to Diane for her seal of disapproval.

"Er, hello... Aren't you going to have a word with your daughter about her outfit today?" asks Trevor, watching Diane searching for something on the table.

"Are you going to have a word with her Sweetie?" she responds.

"Oh no, don't look at me, I ain't getting involved with girl stuff" he nervously sings like he always does.

"Then neither am I... Now where's my shopping notepad?" she responds, only interested in one thing this morning.

"DIANE" he huffs, in total disbelief.

"Are you really telling me you're okay with her leaving the house dressed like she is?" he asks.

"Take no notice of your old fashioned dad, you look lovely Teagan" Diane says, smiling from ear to ear when she finds her notepad under his cereal bowl.

As Trevor stands up ready for work, dazed and confused by his wife's overnight transformation, even Teagan can't believe her ears, because this is the first time her mum has approved. Trevor says goodbye to his wife, his daughter and other daughter from the bottom of the stairs, then leaves for work. Then as the front door closes Hillary comes bouncing down the stairs a reformed character, in her slutty chapped jeans, cleavage hugging top and more importantly, new boots.

"Mum I love them, thank you so much" Hillary chirps, bouncing into the kitchen, as Teagan's face drops through the floor.

"Oh mum that's not fair, how come Hillary got new boots and I didn't?" Teagan grumps, threatening to pull a major strop if the question isn't answered the way she wants it to be.

Very quickly preoccupied Diane turns to Teagan and declares they can talk about it when she comes home from school later, and then have anything she likes.

"Anything she likes? That's not fair mum" Hillary then strops, claiming she only got the boots on her feet and didn't get offered anything she wanted.

"I thought the boots WERE what you wanted Sweetie?" asks Diane, making her valid point.

In order to have neither girl moan at her this morning, Diane decides to tell Hillary she can have another thing later too, then Teagan can pick two things so it evens it up. With both teenagers happy again or more importantly, ready to leave the house, Diane packs them on their way.

"Right, come here notepad" she sings to herself, as the house is finally empty and she knows exactly what she wants to do.

She locks the front door to stop Tia causally walking in, shuts the living room curtains and sits herself down on the sofa, ready to write out a huge shopping list.

Going through a whole list of foods and things the house needs, Diane draws up her list leaving nothing to chance.

"Ten packs of twenty toilet rolls will see us through a good couple of months" she sings to herself.

"No, better make that fourteen packs, as we don't know how long this magic will last" she adds, readjusting her quantities.

With a shopping budget of over £600, something she's never spent in her life, she scrunches up the list, then proceeds to do her thing... She hops, waits... Skips, waits... Then finally before the dizzy kicks in, jumps...

"Here we go" she sings, as her lightheadedness takes effect...


"Thank you very much, please come again" says the cashiers voice minutes later, as she grins, grins a little wider, then slowly opens her eyes.

"I will... Thank-you" she quickly responds, before the smile is completely dampened by yet more confusion...

"Hey, where's my shopping then?" she asks, realising he said those magical words, she is standing at the check-out, but there's no shopping bags.

"Er, Paul over there is taking them out to your car" the guy answers, as though he's only just explained this to her because he did, but she doesn't yet know it.

Diane looks over at the young man called Paul trying to steer four trolleys out of the shop at once, then turns back to the cashier with a smile.

"I've got my receipt, right?" she asks.

"You sure have... Right there in your hand" answers the cashier, growing more and more concerned by her weird questions.

"And I didn't ask for any cash-back, did I?" she asks, tempting him to lose his sanity too.

"No you didn't, why? Would you like some now?" he asks, quickly apologising to the people waiting in the queue.

Diane quickly realises she's just purchased £600 worth of shopping for nothing, then wonders if the cash-back thing would work in the same way. Just as the thought of trying it out races through her mind and she thinks of a figure that she'd like to ask for, her conscience kicks in...

"You know what, I'd better not" she tells him, as she finally leaves the check-out behind her and starts following trolley-boy Paul out towards the car.


With her hoards of supplies, enough for a nuclear war fall-out shelter, it takes Diane longer to carry it all into the house, than it did to do the actual shop. It's not until everything is unloaded in the kitchen and the kitchen itself looks like a supermarket, that she starts to question her sanity again.

"Why the hell would you buy ten tubes of toothpaste?" she asks herself.

"Or more to the point, three jars of Marmite? No-one in the house likes Marmite" she adds, claiming she is losing it and even if she isn't because the shopping trick is real, her items clearly show she is a little...

With this the latest head-fuck screwing up her brain, Diane just to make sure, picks up the phone and starts to dial a number.

"Yeah hello, it's Diane Luck here. Can I make an appointment to see a doctor please?" she says.

"Who would I like to see? A male doctor or female? Er... I will ring you back" she stutters, then crazily hangs up on the surgery receptionist who she had just called.

She places the phone on the table, holds her head in her hands, then starts to think...

"If hanging up on the receptionist wasn't a crazy thing to do, then I guess I'm going mad" she mumbles to herself.

"The cashier thought I was nuts, but I know I'm not... Why the hell am I talking to myself again?" she asks, desperately trying to stop herself from doing the one thing she doesn't want to do, yet feels she's doing it anyway.

Realising now that she needs to visit the doctor for sure, she picks up the phone and dials the surgery again.

"Yeah hello, it's me Mrs Luck again" she says to the receptionist.

"Oh yeah, er... Male or female doctor, that was your question, wasn't it?" she asks, as the receptionist remembers her from three seconds beforehand, then Diane hangs up like a crazy woman for a second time.

"Pull it together Diane, pull it together" she demands of herself, claiming hanging up once was mental, yet twice is insane, as she steps over the five frying spatulas she's purchased this morning.

Before she can lose any more of her marbles, she quickly has an idea and questions the question the receptionist has already asked her twice.

"Male doctor, or female doctor?... I wonder" she whispers to herself, picking her favourite notepad off the table.

"I wonder if this just works for shopping, or every wish I make?" she says.

She finds a place to sit down, writes down the fact she wants to see a female doctor, then rips the wish out of the notepad. She scrunches it up and does her little dance, consisting of a hop, wait... Skip, wait... Then jump... Feeling this idea is her craziest yet, she is the startled when the room begins to spin.

"Oh my god... What if it is everything I wish for?" she slurs, trying not to throw up as the room spins out of control, yet she gets excited.


Just five minutes later, Diane comes round to find herself standing outside the doctor's surgery.

"You're either going to look like a complete fruit-cake or this has happened again" she says to herself entering the building, knowing she didn't finish the conversation with the receptionist over the phone a few minutes ago.

She slowly walks towards the counter and eyes up the said receptionist who could have her sectioned in the next five minutes, if that notepad didn't make the appointment for her.

"Hi, I'm not sure, I think, er... I might have a doctor's appointment" she mumbles, not sounding crazy at all.

"Yes, okay then and what time was your appointment? And what is the name please?" asks the receptionist, able and capable to follow so far.

"Yeah, er... I don't actually remember the time of the appointment, but the name is Mrs Luck... Mrs Diane Luck" she answers, praying that her notepad worked.

Before the young receptionist can question the older woman about the two weird phone-calls she only made minutes ago and the fact she knows nothing was confirmed, she checks her computer anyway.

"Oh..." the receptionist then gasps in shock herself.

"Right on time Mrs Luck... You do have an appointment today" she adds, quickly asking her to take a seat.

Not wanting to read too much into it or get over-excited about it happening with something other than shopping, Diane thanks the receptionist quickly and trots herself over to the waiting area. She quickly spots a seat, then before her bum can touch it, her name is called out.

"Well that doesn't ever happen, does it?" she mumbles to herself, doing a little up and down dance routine next to the seat she was going to take, but doesn't have to now.

The voice from the intercom instructs her to proceed to room four, so she wanders off down the corridor, finally realising she isn't going mad and this thing she's discovered is actually real. She stands herself outside room four, knocks on the door, then realises she doesn't actually know why she's visiting the doctor in the first place.

"Hello Mrs Luck, come in, take a seat, what can I do for you today?" asks the doctors voice, confusing the hell out of her, simply because it's a man's voice doing the talking.

"Er... Sorry... Er... I must have the wrong room" she stutters.

"Are you Mrs Diane Luck? Yes? Then I have your notes right here" he says, claiming she is in the right place, as she, even crazier looking than ever, wobbles towards his desk and takes a seat.

"Were you expecting to see another doctor or something? Because you look a little surprised to see me?" he quickly questions, before asking which doctor her appointment was made with.

"Er... You?" she answers looking puzzled, knowing she didn't actually make the appointment.

The confused doctor strangely enough doesn't pick up on her mental state of mind straight away, yet instead thinks she's being funny so laughs with her. Although Diane isn't laughing, she then tries to work out what the doctor is finding so amusing, then things get even worse when he again asks what her visit is for.

"Er... I... Er... I'm not really sure" she answers.

Although a good old fashioned doctor would by now be able to work out that there's a problem with her mentality, once again this doctor doesn't pick up on anything and instead lets his ego take over...

"I know visiting a male doctor can be unsettling sometimes, but we are as good as female doctors, I can assure you" he explains.

"No matter how good looking the male doctor is" he adds, laughing at his own joke now, which in turn makes her giggle, because she hasn't got a clue what he's talking or laughing about.

"So Mrs Luck, let's put aside I'm a good looking male doctor... What can I help you with today?" he asks.

"Er... Well, what it is, er..." she continues to stutter in a daze.

"This is one for a female doctor, isn't it?" he responds, finally working out she doesn't want to talk to him.

"I am just as good... What is it, a problem with your breasts? A problem with your vagina?" he asks, still trying to reassure her.

On the sound of the word Vagina, Diane snaps out of it in her usual prudish manner and promises her visit has nothing whatsoever to with her female bumps or her thingy below.

"Sorry Mrs Luck, I didn't mean to offend you" he explains, noticing her getting flustered.

"But you can trust me" he adds standing up, walking around his desk and sitting on the edge of it in front of her.

Although him being even closer makes her feel uncomfortable, she still tries to rid her blushes and reject the word vagina from the visit, but the doctor's patience and time is running out.

"You can either tell me what your lady problem is Mrs Luck, or you can arrange another appointment with a female doctor at a later date" he explains.

"That's a good idea" she responds at a chirp, standing up in front of him.

"I will re-arrange at a later date then" she adds, thanking him for his time.

"Not so fast Mrs Luck, not so fast" he sighs, placing a hand on her shoulder, claiming she looks deeply troubled.

"Why don't you lay yourself up on the bed over there and see if I can't help you out first" he suggests.

"Well, yes, I er... I am a little troubled" she answers, before realising she's actually hopping up onto the bed as requested, back in her daze.

Still trying to rid of the word vagina, still trying to work out why she would purchase five frying spatulas and now pondering over why she would be laying there, she then finds her jeans gently being pulled down to reveal her knickers.

"Okay Mrs Luck, what seems to be the problem down here then?" he asks, slowly offering to remove the knickers for her too.

"ER... WHAT? HOW? WHAT ARE YOU DOING?" she yells out in a panic, claiming there's was nothing wrong with her thingy before she walked in and nothing wrong with it now.

"I will only take a quick look" he explains in a soft relaxing tone, pulling at the top of her knickers.

"NO, NO, I DON'T WANT YOU TO TAKE MY PANTS OFF" she screams out, pulling them up, as well as her jeans, getting herself into a tug-of-war with his hand.

Suddenly, the door to the doctor's office bursts open and in walks Tia...

"OH... MY... GOD... Diane, another man? You are a freak" sings Tia all smiles, assuming her friend is up to the seduction thing once again.

"Yes hello, excuse me? But would you mind waiting outside?" huffs the doctor, trying to work out who this female is, or why she's just burst in to his office.

"No, No, I want her... I want her in here inside" panics Diane, still tugging at her knickers.

"FINALLY !!" Tia sighs, taking her friends pants tugging words the wrong way, as she starts to strut towards them.

"No, sorry, but this just isn't good enough... What's going on here?" questions the doctor again, trying to stop Tia from intruding any further.

"This is my friend and she's tugging at her knickers, demanding she

32

wants me inside her" explains seductive Tia, reaching them at the bed.

"So if you're a good little Doctor Spock, you might be a lucky boy and get a three way out of this" she adds.

As Diane tries to inform her friend there's no sex to be had and the doctor panics about his intact professional reputation, all three of them are doing different things... As the doctor demands they both leave his room, its Tia stopping Diane from pulling up her jeans fully now.

"Tia, Tia, stop... I didn't mean it that way" Diane pleads, finally pulling free, jumping off the bed and hitching her jeans back into place.

"First you seduce a delivery guy, then it's a fucking doctor... All without me" Tia responds, grumbling at her selfish friend.

"Tia, Tia, we weren't doing anything" explains Diane, as her voice reaches a high-pitched panic station level.

"Yeah... So why did I walk in and find HIS hands down YOUR knickers?" grunts Tia, making up her own version of what she thought she saw again.

"I was just examining your partner's vagina, that's all" the doctor butts in, still demanding they leave, assuming they are lesbians now.

"Oh no, we're not... You know, we're not, er..." stutters Diane, blushing again now at something else the doctor is saying, yet not being able to say it fully herself.

"Just examining her vagina indeed" Tia interrupts, looking the doctor up and down with dirty fuck-me eyes, then calling him a pervert.

"If you were just examining her pussy, what for exactly?" she huffs, knowing if her friend did have a problem down there, she'd already know about it.

This time it's the doctors turn to blush and stutter, as the question seems far too confusing to answer.

"Er... Well, er..." he stutters, looking for an answer.

"Er... Well, er..." Tia mocks him.

"Then I guess you wouldn't mind examining my pussy as well then babes?" she adds, leaping up onto the bed, parting her legs, hitching up her already short skirt and showing him what she had for breakfast.

"LOOK !!... I don't know what's going on here, but you've really got to leave" the doctor grunts, trying his best not to look at Tia's vagina, although he's just looked at least four times.

"Come on Doc, show us your cock" Tia sings, placing her hand between her legs.

"Ple..assseee, tell me what's wrong with my vagina Doctor, I just can't stop it getting wet" she adds, teasing him to the point of collapse.

With that grabs hold of her friend, then drags her off the bed. She quickly apologises to the doctor, then marches her sexually frustrated friend out of the room, closing the door behind her.

"What's wrong with you Diane? Why can't we ever have any fun?... You do know he's going to sit behind his desk and play with his HUGE cock now, don't you?" groans Tia, suggesting she can let go of her arm now, desperate to show her disappointment.

Without another word said, Diane strolls out of the doctor's surgery and blanks her friend completely.

"Oh I get it... The silent treatment, is it?" Tia calls out, following.

"Just because I walked in and ruined your affair with the doctor" she adds, putting her usual two and two together and coming up with a sexual 69.

Although Diane doesn't want to talk to her friend, she knows too much has happened today for her not to broadcast it everywhere. She turns back to her, demands she go home, then promises she will explain all in the morning.

"Is that all as in ALL? Or all as in all, but I will miss out ALL the gory details, all?" asks Tia.

"I will tell you EVERYTHING... Now not another word, okay?" responds Diane, making Tia promise, to zip her mouth shut.

As silent Tia agrees to do what she is told and the two girls plan to depart in different directions, Diane realises there's something that's going to bug her all night long, so calls Tia back. Unfortunately, Tia plays up to the challenge set and buttons her mouth closed tighter, implying she isn't going to answer, then continues to walk away.

"But why were you at the doctors in the first place?" calls Diane, getting a blank for her troubles.

### NOTHING !!

"No seriously Tia... What were you there for? And how did you know I was in that room?" Diane asks, chasing her friend up the street.

Finally Tia stops, smiles, then sarcastically un-zips her mouth.

"Shut your mouth Tia, open it... Don't say another word Tia, answer my question" she sings out, mocking confused Diane, still waiting for an answer.

"Why were YOU at the doctors?" growls Diane in a friendly manner.

"I couldn't get into your house this morning because someone had locked the door, so I followed you?" answers playful Tia.

"You followed me?" responds Diane, knowing she didn't actually walk to the doctors.

"Yeah I followed you" answers Tia.

"How is that possible?" Diane mumbles under her breath.

With that Tia shakes her head in her friend's direction, tells her she's losing it, then shows her how with her legs sarcastically, as she walks away.

# CHAPTER 5
## SPATULA

Unable to work out why this notepad thing is happening to her, why she has found herself in two different sexual encounters today with different men... Why the notepad thing didn't work for the female doctor request, yet did book an appointment... Then why Tia keeps showing up every time a man is involved, Diane is really confused !!

So confused in-fact that after leaving Tia at the surgery, she's managed to walk around random streets thinking to herself for a whole three hours without realising it. Although she's been completely dazed throughout the marathon walk, nothing has made sense and she still doesn't know anything.

"BUGGER !!..." she then huffs, landing on planet Earth for the third time today, realising time has passed and everyone should be at home by now.

She then quickly gets disheartened and wonders why none of her family have tried to ring her, as she pulls her phone out of her pocket.

"Double Bugger !!" she huffs again, noticing six missed calls from home.

Now knowing her family are home, worried about her or more importantly questioning how the kitchen turned into a supermarket, she dreads making her way home.

Half an hour later as if the day couldn't possibly get any more confusing, she walks through her front door and finds the kitchen has magically tidied itself and everything has been put into place. Whilst she sticks the kettle on and wonders if the notepad has done this for her too, it's then dropped on her like a bombshell...

"Hey Honey-bun, where have you been?" asks Trevor walking into the room.

"And where did all the shopping come from?" he asks.

Without an "Er" or a random stuttered response, Diane does the only sane thing she can think of doing at that moment in time...

"WOW!!... Why all the bloody questions? Can I get in first and have a cup of coffee please?" she explodes in a soft rage, knocking poor gob-smacked Trevor off his feet.

"Er, yeah, sure?... Is everything okay?" he asks, stumbling back against the counter in shock.

With that Hillary in her new boots and Teagan ready to demand presents, race into the room too.

"Mum, can I tell you what I want now?" asks Teagan, standing there in a long shirt and nothing else.

"Mum, where did all the shopping come from?" asks Hillary at the same time.

"Please tell me you didn't go to school looking like that Teagan" sighs Trevor, looking at his daughter, then at his wife.

"Did she Diane?" he asks, firing a third question his wife's way within seconds.

Diane stands facing the kitchen sink, takes a sip of coffee, counts to ten, then slowly turns around.

"Teagan, leave your list on the table and I will make it happen... Hillary, I had a little flutter on the horses today and won, therefore bought the shopping with the winnings... By the way, please leave a note of what else you want me to get you on the table too... And Trevor, I've been down to the bank to put the rest of my winnings into a safe place" she explains, without taking a single breath.

"HOW MUCH DID YOU WIN?" all three of them ask in unison.

Realising this is a question she didn't expect to answer or more to the point, didn't have a lie in store for, she simply mumbles out the words

"Not much" and that's everyone taken care of...

As Seventeen year old Hillary writes down the name of the skirt she wants, she kisses her mother on the cheek and goes up to her room. Fifteen year old Teagan watches her older sister, mimics her actions and does exactly the same with her list.

"And what did you get me then?" Trevor asks with a big smile on his face, watching his daughters leave the room like its Christmas day or something.

Diane thinks about it quickly, doesn't have a clue, then opens a cupboard and pulls out one of the five frying pan spatulas she sort of purchased today.

"A spatula?" questions confused looking Trevor, trying to hold his smile.

"Oh no, not just any old spatula, but one you can..." she answers, uncharacteristically flirting with her eyes, walking over to him, then whispering something suggestive in his ear to finish her sentence.

"I can do what to you with it, where?" he stammers in shock again, with a face that says forget Christmas because all his birthdays have come at once.

"Well what are we waiting for? Let's go to bed" he sings sounding so excited, he doesn't for a second realise she didn't actually get him anything or that the clock on the wall states it's only six o'clock in the evening.

Unwilling to take no for an answer and seeing how his wife never initiates sex, Trevor is already galloping half way up the stairs, when he calls back for her...

"ARE YOU COMING THEN?" he calls, making more noise with his stamping feet, than his voice.

"Oh and don't forget to bring some oil up for the spatula fun too" he adds, reaching the top of the stairs, then bumping into his eldest daughter.

"Eww... That's gross dad, gross !!" gasps Hillary, wearing a disproving frown.

"Er, no, I... You don't understand... Your mum... I, er..." he stutters, not knowing whether to be embarrassed by his loud request or the fact his daughter knows what it's for.

"I'd like to say too much information father dear, but let's just drop it, shall we?" she responds, claiming what her parents do in the bedroom, should always stay in THEIR bedroom.

With that Hillary marches back off to her room, leaving poor Trevor slightly bewildered on the stairs waiting for Diane.

"Sorry, did you ask for oil?" calls Diane from the bottom of the stairs, holding a bottle of sunflower oil in her hand.

"You know what, let's leave the oil" he responds, asking how long she's going to be downstairs for, realising the moment for him has just passed.

Giving him the extra time needed to refuel his libido, Diane confirms that she's got a few things to do downstairs first. Diane walks back into the kitchen, knowing she's got a lot of information to process, but doesn't know where to begin with it all. She sits down at the table and plays with the spatula for a few minutes, trying to work things out. Strangely enough and just like her marathon walk, she ends up sitting there for a full two hours unnoticed, just gazing into space... Unnoticed that is until Trevor realises he's still upstairs on his own and wonders where she is now his interest has finally sparked up again.

"DIANE, are you coming to bed tonight?" he calls from the landing.

"Eww Dad, what's wrong with you?" huffs a voice right behind him, be it of his youngest daughter now, Teagan.

"What? I only asked your mum if she's coming to bed" he responds, trying to act as innocent as he can, knowing himself it wasn't an innocent question, yet it should have sounded like one.

"Yeah and the only time you call mum up to bed is when you're going to you know... Make the bed spring noises" says his daughter, sending shudders of fear through his body, before leaving him standing there like Hillary did hours ago.

"Sorry... What was that?" calls Diane from the bottom of the stairs.

"I was just asking..." he responds, checking around for his daughters, before speaking.

"No, don't worry, it doesn't matter" he adds, letting his libido deflate for the second time.

Unfortunately this time, Diane knows what he's asking, without him actually asking and surprises him by confirming she'll be up in a few minutes. Just like that his sexual interest returns and he dances on the spot like a teenager on a promise. That's until seconds later; Hillary walks past him on her way to the bathroom, notices what he's doing and gives him another disapproving look.

"What's wrong with you girls tonight?" he huffs, before his eldest can have a go at him again.

"I go days without seeing you both, then every time I speak to your mother, there you appear" he adds.

Without words Hillary gives him a strange look, and returns to her room after using the bathroom, then offers to shut her door.

"Oh and dad..." she whispers from the crack in the door, before it's fully closed on him.

"Try and keep the groaning down to a minimum please" she adds.

Refusing to get embarrassed by his daughters request, Trevor sighs and promises to help Diane from moaning too loudly tonight...

"I wasn't talking about mum, I was talking about you" she responds, knowing she's about to deliberately shatter any hope of his sexual interest peaking again this evening.

Dejected Trevor heads into the bedroom, where he knows in a few minutes time he must satisfy or at least entertain his wife for the first time in weeks, yet his heart or any other body parts needed aren't interested again. He pulls down his boxer shorts, positions his naked body on the bed taking up a sexy, towards the door pose, that looks more like a pose for a room full of painting artists.

"They're going to walk in, aren't they? They're going to walk in" he mumbles to himself, still trying to look hot enough for his oncoming wife, yet more worried about his intrusive daughters walking in.

With that he panics, realises his two daughters must NEVER see him like this and dives under the covers. With only seconds to spare, he shuffles, twist and turns, but he just can't resume a sexy pose, not that the one before would look remotely arousing to anyone. As the door begins to open, he lies there in what can only be described as a constipated chicken pose, yet is saved by his wife not looking any sexier walking in. As she holds the spatula up in front of her, looking herself like she's about to perform an anal examination on him with it, she walks towards him on the bed. He looks at her and she looks at him, then they both suddenly agree this isn't such a good idea after all.

"Shall we just er, leave it tonight?" he suggests, realising the mood has definitely past for him now.

"Yeah, well, if you're... Yeah, if you're sure" she stutters in response, finally lowing the spatula.

"I have actually got a tiny headache coming on" she adds, although she doesn't.

"Yeah and I've got to be up early for work tomorrow anyway" he sighs, as they both try to justify not having sex again with each-other tonight.

As a more relieved Diane joins him on the bed, both of them realise their sex life isn't what it used to be and although both of them hold onto fake smiles, they just know something is seriously missing in their marriage.

"We could you know, do it really fast if you want to you know, do it?" she says sliding underneath the sheets, knowing only too well that the smile on his face isn't the smile of a happy man.

"We could, yeah, er... Yeah, we could" he stutters, not wanting to let her down, although he knows himself it'll take a box full of very strong boner pills to make him stand up now.

With the invitation offered sympathetically and accepted reluctantly, Diane removes her pyjama bottoms and takes up the missionary position, which simply requires her legs to be parted. Trevor slowly but surely mounts his wife's body, grunts and groans as he moves, then sticks his hand between the bed and the wall for good measure.

"What are you doing? Why are you trapping your hand behind there?" she asks in a confused wife sounding drone.

"Bed springs" he grunts, wedging his arm in too and struggling with the position.

"Don't want to hear the bed springs" he grunts again, failing to explain properly.

In what looks to be a normal man and wife sexual missionary position, the only thing sexy in the room is the old VHS pornographic video tape they used to watch, which has decayed at the back of the wardrobe, yet is still sexier than them put together.

"Take your hand out of there" she grunts at him, as she gets his other elbow in her face.

"I won't be able to get hard if the bed starts making noises" he huffs and puffs, not realising that he's putting more effort into the gap in the wall, than his wife waiting for sex.

"Well maybe if you stopped rubbing the wall and touched your wife for a change, you'd be more interested in what we are doing" she huffs, starting to get the hump with him.

"MM-mm, nothing like your dirty talking skills to turn me on" he grunts back, taking offence himself.

With that he pulls his arm out of the gap, reaches down below the sheets as requested and runs his hand up her leg, before shuddering in shock, then stopping dead in his tracks.

"Oh yeah, sorry... I would have shaved my legs if I knew we had this planned tonight" she responds.

"Shaved?" he huffs.

"Your leg hair feels longer than mine... You would need a lawnmower to trim them" he adds, finally really offending her.

Without needing to move his hand away from her hairy thighs himself, she reaches down, pushes him away, then slams shut her legs, forcing him off her. As he falls to his own side of the bed, both of them are in a foul mood and neither of them want sex, ironically not for the first time this evening.

"What happened to us?" he sighs, looking up at the ceiling.

"We used to be so good together" he adds, realising the moment has FINALLY past for good now.

Unwilling to turn and face him, she just looks forward, then claims they got old.

"Old?" he shudders.

"I didn't get older, you got old... I've always wanted sex, it's you that turned into the p..." he adds.

"Go on, say it" she demands, realising he was going to say the horrid P word.

Trevor straight away realises what's good for him, so remains silent.

"Say it... Call me what you were about to call me" she demands again.

He has a very quick think to himself, then tries to think of any P word that would sound remotely passable.

"I said it was you that turned into the p... p..." he stutters, still trying to think fast.

"Yeah !!" she growls softly, yet harsh enough.

"P... p... Into the PRETTY old person" he answers, finally coming up

43

with something.

As though it wouldn't have been offensive enough to really call her a prude, Trevor soon realises that he might as well have called her it, based on the fact his new P word hasn't gone down too well either.

"That's crap Trevor, crap" she grunts, pulling the sheets away from him.

"You were going to call me a prude, weren't you? Come on say it, tell me the truth" she demands, claiming if he doesn't, he'll be sleeping on the sofa tonight.

Not wanting to believe his once highly sexual wife has turned into the prude he sees before him, Trevor refuses to call her it and with that drags himself off the bed.

"I guess I will be sleeping on the sofa then" he sighs, putting on his pants.

"Yeah that's right, go then" she huffs, pumping up her pillows with aggression.

"Walk away... Go on walk away... You're nothing but a coward Trevor Luck, a COWARD" she adds, raising her voice as she watches him plan to leave the room.

"A coward?" he responds, stopping at the door.

"I'm not the one claiming I can spank someone's backside with a spatula, then bottle it... And I'm not the one that goes to bed expecting sex, covered in more hair than a fucking hairy footballer" he adds, slamming the door behind him, determined to get the final word.

Determined he's not getting the final word, she leaps off the bed in her pants, races towards the door and opens it...

"Yeah, well I'm not the one that can't say the bloody word prude, am I?" she calls out after him, then slamming the door on him this time.

As dejected Diane strolls across the bedroom and slides back into bed, the bedroom door opens again...

"Prude, prude, you're a fucking PRUDE" he yells out across the room, going to slam the door, then realises his daughters could be listening from their rooms, so closes it gently.

Within seconds this cat and mouse game reaches new heights, as Diane leaps out of bed again and opens the bedroom door for the second time...

"If you want to call me a prude, JUST CALL ME ONE" she yells out, before noticing he's just outside the door himself, hasn't gone downstairs yet and is begging her to be quiet.

With that he informs her in silent mode that the commotion is going to disturb their daughters, then claims quietly that he did in-fact just call her one.

"Yeah, well you're an inconsiderate sexist, who won't do anything unless you have a son... Dic... Wan... Turd" she whispers in an aggressive tone.

"Unshaven, non-sexual, BORE" he whispers back at her.

"You're the bore, I've done plenty of sexy stuff, thank you very much" she answers, before claiming he hasn't.

"What, like in... 1946?" he spits back at a whisper, feeling this is one battle he's going to win for sure.

"Well at least I've done stuff" she huffs, claiming it's a lot more than he's ever done.

"Oh yeah, like what?" he asks, not impressed unless she can actually say or prove it.

"Er, well, er..." she stutters.

"Er, well, er... NOTHING !!" he mocks her, tempting his voice to get louder than the whisper.

Claiming she doesn't want to say anything sexual out on the landing in-case the girls do hear, she insists if he wants the answers, he needs to step back into the bedroom. Within seconds they are both back in the bedroom, where Trevor feels like his prudish wife might actually say something of sexual interest for the first time ever.

"Come on then, let's hear all the things you've done, that I haven't" he huffs, not sounding impressed at all, yet secretly hoping he will be soon.

"Er, yeah, er... Well I've had sex in a car before" she confesses, claiming that isn't the behaviour of a prudish person.

"Er yeah, with me" he responds, not feeling impressed at all yet.

"That I initiated by the way, I pulled the car over in that picnic area and I did all the humping" he adds, claiming it hardly puts her up there with a sexy porn star.

Diane quickly thinks to herself, comes up with the thing she and Tia did together years ago and knows this is porn star level for sure.

"Okay then, I once... I er... Back in my school days, I er..." she

45

stutters, realising although she can wipe the smirk off his face, she can't actually say it.

"I er, you er.. School er" he mocks again.

"I... Well when I say I, I mean Tia and I, er..." she responds, forcing her darkest secret out.

"You and Tia fucked each-other, yeah I know that... Tell me something I don't already know" he responds, not only knocking her sideways, but off her feet literally and onto the bed.

As she sits there gob-smacked by his confession and desperate to ask how he knows, nothing but more stuttering nonsense comes out of her mouth. Instead of asking the question she wants answered so much, she instead thinks things through quickly and realises she should have won this battle after all anyway. Before he can say another word, she asks if that deems herself fit enough not to be a prude.

"Yeah it does" he answers.

"But the fact you've kept it to yourself all these years... The fact it happened all those years ago... Then no it doesn't" he adds, taking it back straight away.

Feeling a little lost now, she sits there trying to work it out...

"Now if you'd have said, me and Tia fucked last week, I would have said..." he says.

"You've committed adultery? You've been dishonest, disloyal and cheated?" she answers for him.

"I would have said that's hot" he answers, tempting even more confusion.

"What? How? I don't unders... How is that not cheating?" she asks, stuttering again.

"It can't be considered cheating if I let you do it" he answers, all of a sudden losing his aggressive tone and actually looking like he wants sex again now.

"But I... How? I don't think I like women that way" she stutters.

"Neither does your friend, but it wouldn't stop her, would it?" he asks.

"I bet Tia would take a bit of dick over a vagina any day of the week, but it doesn't stop her having fun, does it?" he asks, firing yet another question her way.

A few more stutters later... A few more strange pulled faces, confused

Diane finally has something to say on the matter.

"How the bloody hell do you know what MY friend Tia is really like?" she asks, not actually asking or responding in the way he imagined it in his head.

Being careful and answering with honesty, he declares Tia's been in his life just as much as his wife's and should also know her well enough.

"You know, just because she's your friend, it doesn't mean she hasn't been in my life too" he explains.

"Oh yeah, how do you mean, in your life?" Diane blurts out, instantly getting the wrong end of the stick and becoming somewhat jealous.

"We are man and wife... We share a life together... Your best friend is Tia... Meaning she's a part of my life too" he responds, stating the obvious, although not obvious enough to her all these years.

"So you've always known about our fling then, have you?" she asks, finally understanding and coming round.

"I've known since day one" he answers, with a loving smile on his face.

"You wouldn't believe how many times I've bashed the bish..." he adds, before suddenly stopping, noticing her face has dramatically changed...

"GO ON..." she growls.

"Er... I mean, er..." he responds, taking this his opportunity to catch up in the stuttering stakes.

As he stands there without a shovel to dig himself out of his hole, she weighs it all up...

"Let me get this straight" she says, with a smile that looks like a bomb about to explode.

"You've known about us for years, didn't tell me and lied about it... And you've constantly been bash... Mastur... Fantasising about it too?" she asks, magically turning it round on him.

"Er... I..." he stutters some more, knowing it's all about right, but it sounding really bad for him now.

"You lying... Cheating... Son-of-a-bitch" she erupts.

"Thinking about MY friend in THAT way, you DISGUSTING PIG" she adds, standing up and whacking her fist against his chest.

"But I... It was you that..." he tries to defend himself, whilst being forced towards the door, then suddenly gives up...

"Oh you know what? Forget it" he adds, making a bolt for the door, claiming he's going to sleep downstairs anyway.

"GOOD, YOU PIG !!" she responds, claiming she doesn't want him in her bed anyway.

"Yeah but you wouldn't mind if it was your lesbian friend, would you?" he snaps back, opening the door.

"I told you, I don't think I'm like that" she responds, picking up a photo frame, ready to launch it at him in anger.

"You know, I wouldn't mind if you said YOU'RE NOT LIKE THAT, because then you'd know" he says, standing in the doorway.

"But you THINKING YOU'RE NOT LIKE THAT, just proves one thing... You don't know because you're such a FUCKING PRUDE" he bellows out, as the photo frame comes flying towards him and he slams the door just in time, pleased he got the final word at least.

He didn't...

"For your information, I ain't a bloody prude... I would sleep with a man who wanted to touch me and maybe I will find out if I like women or not" she calls out, watching him walk down the stairs.

"Well when you know what you are, do me a favour and let me know too... PRUDE" he yells back at her.

"Enjoy the sofa, PIG !!" she calls back, as their final word game persists.

"I WILL... BITCH" he yells back.

"Yeah, you'll be back upstairs when you want sex again... USER" she calls out.

"Not until you shave your MANLY LEGS or find out if you're a LESBIAN or not... PRUDE" he responds, heading into the living room and out of sight.

"Back for sex when YOU NEED IT or are bashing yourself thinking about TIA... SMALL MINDED, ARSE... WILLY" she bellows out, trying to keep her voice down, but not doing a good job.

As Trevor disappears into the living room for the night and Diane back into the bedroom, the couple both realise things have been this way for a while now and think the other one will back down first.

## 2 MINUTES LATER...

As Diane gets comfy in bed to process her crazy day, she then watches the bedroom door open again and in walk a lost looking Trevor.

"Wow, that must be a record... A full two minutes downstairs" she mocks him, claiming there's no way she's going to forgive him that quickly, still out of breath from her previous outburst.

"Forgive me? I'm not the one that slept with someone else of the same gender... I'm not the one that didn't tell her husband all these years... And I'm not the one that's a fucking PRUDE" he responds.

"If that's your idea of apologising Trevor, then we have a big problem" she huffs from the bed, as he continues to stand at the door. With that he slowly approaches the bed...

"Don't you dare come over here. I don't want to sleep next to you" she demands, as he completely ignores her.

"If you think you're going to get sex, whilst you think about my best friend, you are very much mistaken" she adds, unable to work out why he's still coming towards the bed.
The question is then answered when he grabs a pillow, tosses it on the floor and throws himself down on top of it...

"I thought you were sleeping downstairs?" she huffs, working out that he's going to sleep on the floor instead.
He sits back up, looks at her, then frowns...

"Whilst I was up here waiting for you for to deliver your non-existent spatula idea for hours this evening, what were you doing downstairs?" he asks.

"Ironing" she answers.

"And where did you leave all that ironing?" he asks.

"On the sofa" she answers.

"And would it be okay if I moved the said ironing from the sofa to sleep on?" he asks.

"If you want to re-fold it, yes" she answers.

"And that's why I am on the fucking floor... PRUDE" he huffs, making his point, then throwing himself down to settle for the night.

"En-JOY the FLOOR th-en" she sings, before calling him a lazy pig.

# CHAPTER 6
## SHOES

It's yet another morning in the Luck family household and although things erupted last night between the married couple, things have settled down a lot since then. As Trevor searches through the cupboards and is somewhat spoilt for choice for a change, he can't make up his mind what to have.

"Teagan, Hillary, times getting on. Let's get a wriggle on, shall we" Diane calls from the bottom of the staircase, as though everything is normal.
She walks back into the kitchen and her eyes meet Trevor's for the first time this morning...

"I think maybe we... I, said a few things I didn't really mean last night" she says.

"Yeah, I think I did too... How about we just pretend it didn't, you know..." responds Trevor.

"Happen?" she guesses, with a smile on her face, finishing his sentence.

"Yeah, happen" he responds with a smile too.
As the day threatens to turn into yet another normal day for Trevor, Diane secretly has a million things on her mind. How she's going to silence Tia about the two men non-seduction thing yesterday... How she plans to do more shopping today without it being noticed by her

family... And if she's completely honest with herself, still hurt by the P word used a lot last night.

"Morning mum, morning dad" sings Hillary, walking into the room.

"So when is my new skirt going to turn up then?" she asks her mum, clearly only happy about one thing.

Before Diane can turn to her daughter, in walks Teagan looking like a slut ready for school, asking the same question.

"Oh come on Teagan, please tell me that's what you wore to bed last night and you aren't going to school like that" sighs Trevor, looking his youngest daughter up and down, then at Diane for a disapproving comment, then realising she isn't going to give one.

"Don't listen to him Teagan" chirps big sister Hillary, making her own breakfast.

"If dad questions your outfit again, just say the words oil and spatula" she adds, giggling about their meeting on the landing last night. With that beaten Trevor notices his wife turn away looking embarrassed, realises she isn't going to back him up, so forgets his breakfast and gives her a kiss on the cheek to say goodbye.

"Eww, get a room... Not the landing or the kitchen" giggles Hillary, loving to wind her father up as much as she is.

"Girls, love you... See you this evening" Trevor says keeping his British stiff upper lip in place, pretending it isn't bothering him.

Just as the three women in his life watch him walk down the hallway, he stops and returns to the kitchen with something on his mind. Brushing aside Hillary's comment about him forgetting his bottle of oil, he asks if this little purple patch with money could stretch to him having something.

"Anything you want. Just name it" answers Diane, really pleased he's asking.

"I'd love to catch up with the boys, have a few drinks tonight" he explains, claiming eight notes should do it.

"Er, yeah, well, you see..." Diane begins to stutter, knowing herself the shopping might be free, but cash itself isn't.

"I thought you said we had a lot of money?" he asks, looking confused.

"In-fact, I remember you saying you'd just been to the bank last night to make a deposit" he adds.

Knowing it's all another lie, Diane quickly explains that after Hillary's new skirt and Teagan's new boots and mobile phone there won't actually been any money left.

"Ah..." sighs Trevor.

"Oh well, never mind... See you later" he adds, giving his wife another kiss telling her not to worry, then leaving the house.


Once the girls have left the house five minutes later, Diane turns all her attention to Tia, who is expected to turn up in the next hour. She knows she has no explanation about the two men yesterday and really wants to tell her that Trevor knows about their fling, but has only one idea to stop her friend from talking. She reaches for her magical notepad, turns the laptop on and orders her friend the most expensive pair of shoes possible.

"Okay magical notepad, please work for me today" she prays to herself, doing her famous Hop, skip and jump routine.

As soon as she lands the jump, the room begins to spin. She sits herself down like an old pro and waits for it to pass. Two minutes later the job is done, the shoes should be on their way and bang on time as Tia walks in.

"Okay Miss Seduction in a towel, let's hear your all, tell me the whole story then" sings Tia, bouncing into the kitchen, getting straight down to the promised point.

Diane needs to stall her friend for at least half an hour, so insists they have a cup of coffee before talking. As the kettle boiling takes five minutes off the wait, Diane quickly asks how she likes the new perfume she got her yesterday.

"You rushed off so fast, that I didn't know if it helped you" she explains.

Although suspicious Tia already knows Diane is trying to change the subject, being the woman she is, she just can't help but boast...

"Let's just say, another day like yesterday and I will need another bottle of the stuff" answers Tia, claiming successful isn't the word for it.

"You've already used half a bottle?" gasps Diane, faking a shocked response in order to stall time some more.

"Half a bottle in exchange for sixteen perfectly good orgasms... Well worth the usage I'd say" responds gloating Tia, reliving yesterday's notches in her head.

"Sixteen?" gasps Diane again, still faking it up, still sounding interested, yet over-doing it slightly by asking what the orgasm of the day was and who with.

"Okay Miss All as in all, yet giving nothing and changing the subject, what's going on?" Tia barks playfully, knowing something isn't right.

"Any time we talk sex you prudishly change the subject, so why this morning do you want all the gory details?" she asks.

"Just interested" answers Diane, trying not to look guilty, whilst looking up at the clock.

"Interested my wet slash, you lying bitch... Come on, what's going on?" Tia barks again.

Knowing there's a good fifteen minutes until the delivery turns up and realising she isn't going to face the ordeal of listening to her friends mucky sex stories, Diane knows there's only one thing left for it...

"Trevor knows" she says, blushing at the thought of it, or in-fact confessing it.

"Trevor knows what?" questions Tia, not following.

"Knows that you bought me some perfume yesterday? Knows that I love sex? What?" she asks, adamant she needs more from her friend than those words.

Finally Diane realising this should see off the final fifteen minutes, so informs her friend that Trevor knows about their fling years ago.

"OH... MY... GOD" Tia blurts out in shock, mouth wide open.

"Well don't look at me, I didn't tell him... I wouldn't, I couldn't... I mean, I could have many times... Many times over the years, but didn't... No, definitely didn't... Not me, no way" she adds, getting herself into a right tizzy about it, feeling she needs to defend herself without an actual accusation being made.

"Tia its okay" says the soothing tone of Diane's voice.

"I said it wasn't me... I wouldn't, I couldn't... I shouldn't... I shouldn't have... Oh my god, was it me? Did I get drunk and say something stupid?" Tia continues to panic.

"Tia" responds Diane, trying to calm her down or at least get her attention.

"Did I come over drunk last night? Oh my god, did I really say something? Was he okay when I told him? Does he hate me? Did it turn him on? Oh please tell me we didn't have a threesome that I've forgotten about" Tia panics some more.

"TIA !!" calls Diane, finally getting her full attention.

"It was me... Well sort of me... He knew, he's known about it for years" she adds, as Tia takes a seat at the kitchen table and tries her best to take it all in.

"You told him? But why? And what do you mean, sort of? You either did or you didn't?" questions a calmer Tia, finally stopping to take breath and a sip of coffee.

Diane explains without going into any detail about the spatula, that she and Trevor talked openly about last night and it just all came out.

"OH... MY... GOD... Trevor knows" Tia responds, finally taking it in this time, slowing her talking speed down, then strangely asking how she'll ever face him again.

"The same way you face him everyday" answers Diane, slightly confused by the question.

Although Tia has managed to take the information in twice now, it's as though she needs to take it in once more, before it will truly sink in, then asks how he took it.

"Okay, I guess" answers Diane.

"You guess? What does that mean?" huffs Tia.

"Is he all smiles about it? Did you have sex after and fantasise about me? Oh my god, that's why my ears were burning last night" she adds, threatening to get in a tizzy again.

"He's fine and no we didn't have sex" responds Diane, trying to make this part honest at least.

Finally Tia does explode and panic some more...

"How can you say he's fine, yet you didn't have sex? If he was fine, he would have cum up your tunnel faster than the Gatwick Express... Oh my god, he wasn't fine, was he? He hates me now, doesn't he? Oh I see, he wants me gone, we can't be friends any more... That's why you've called me round, isn't it?" she panics.

"Tia, I didn't call you round. You just turn up here every day" explains Diane.

**DING DONG !!**

"Saved by the door" sighs Diane.

"Saved by the door, what does that mean? Oh no, is it him? Is it Trevor? Is this a honey-pot trap thingy, where he expects me and you to do it again? Wow, I haven't been with another woman in years, how do I know I still enjoy it? Oh please tell me he hasn't brought a camcorder with him? Tell me he doesn't want to record us?" panics Tia, threatening to get emotionally tearful.

"It's just a delivery Tia... it's okay" says Diane, trying to reassure her friend or at least stop her talking.

"Delivery? Delivery? Is that your seduction gone wrong delivery guy coming back? Oh my god, he's Trevor's friend, isn't he? They've both come with friends to punish and gang rape me, haven't they?" Tia continues, now strangely threatening to go into extreme fantasy panic mode.

"It's the delivery of my new pair of shoes Tia, nothing else" explains Diane, walking towards the front door.

"Shoes? Then why didn't you just say that DI...ANE" responds Tia, instantly breaking out of her tizzy at the word shoes and following her friend down the hallway.

As Diane answers the front door, signs for the secret half an hour magical delivery, then walks back into the kitchen with the parcel, Tia follows her like a lost puppy.

"OH... MY... GOD" sings Tia, as the parcel is opened to reveal the world's most expensive pair of black shoes.

"How? You can't afford? How? These are like eight hundred quid" stutters shocked Tia, as Diane sits at the table, then pretends to try them on, secretly knowing they aren't going to fit.

"Oh darn, I've gone and ordered the wrong size" says Diane, playing out her plan to perfection.

"Well you better get them changed then. They must have cost a fortune" responds Tia, totally mesmerised by the shoes, before claiming she'd give up the penis to own them.

"Why would I order them in a size FIVE, if my foot is a four?" Diane fakes a groan, waiting for Tia to catch on.

"My size being a four... YOURS A SIZE FIVE?" she questions, trying desperately to make it obvious now.

As Diane sits there looking right into her friends glazed eyes, it takes another twenty seconds before she does catch on...

56

"Did you say a five?" asks Tia.

"Yeah, silly me eh..." responds Diane.

"You don't have to say yes, but could I just try them on?" asks Tia, explaining she loves them to death and doesn't believe she'll ever get to put something on her feet that beautiful ever in her life.

With that Diane's job is done and with the confession that Trevor knows about their fling, Tia is silenced. Tia slips the new shoes on her feet, then races towards the mirror in the hallway to get a better look. She lifts them, she admires them, she does a few spins in them, then for some reason, begins to cry.

"What's wrong with you now?" asks confused Diane.

"I've just never seen a pair of shoes so beautiful" Tia sobs, claiming she needs to take them off before she falls in love with them.

"Have them" responds Diane, standing right next to her.

"Look at them... Oh my god, If I owned these, I'd be the happiest woman alive" Tia says, not hearing her friend at all.

"Have them" Diane chirps again.

"Could you just imagine how many men I would..."

"What did you just say?" asks Tia.

"I said, they're yours" chirps Diane, nothing but big smiles.

"Now don't you play with me girl... A joke like this would make someone suicidal, you know" barks playful yet shocked Tia.

It's not until Diane has said it for a fifth time that Tia realises she's not playing and means every word.

"But they must have cost you a fortune" gasps Tia, before asking how much they were.

"They're worth seven hundred and twenty-two pounds, but I got them for nothing, so they're yours" explains Diane.

"You got them for nothing? What are they, stolen? I don't do stolen goods babes" huffs Tia, instantly taking a disliking to them if they are, but knowing herself that she'd take them anyway, knocked off or not.

Once Diane has told another little fib about a cousin over in America that gets things for free and knows she should have started here in the first place, Tia buys it, then brashly asks if this cousin has a black dress to match her new shoes.

"I'm sure she does" giggles Diane, placing the laptop in front of Tia and requesting she find one on the internet she likes.

Tia doesn't take six years about her decision and immediately picks out an eighty pound dress she likes the look of.

"Now I'm sure your cousin won't have this exact dress, but something like it will do" explains Tia, showing her friend the dress of choice.

"You'll be surprised what my cousin can get her hands on" giggles Diane, knowing the dress on the screen is the one Tia will have.

Before demanding Tia stick the kettle on or making the excuse that she needs to phone her cousin in the other room, Diane makes it clear that this is a one off. Although she would do anything for Tia and give her anything, she doesn't want to become her friend's personal shopping basket. With a little help from Diane's make-believe cousin and the fact she doesn't want to take advantage, the deal is done. As Diane rushes into the next room to make her hop, skip and jump phone-call, Tia supposed to be making the coffee sits at the kitchen table, mesmerised by her new shoes.

Five minutes later and after her little spin around the living room, Diane returns to the kitchen and announces that her make-believe cousin does have the dress in question and it'll be here tomorrow.

After what is the longest friendship hug in the world, with no lesbian thoughts from either of the women, Tia and her new life-partner shoes, head home.


Later that night, hours after tea and after the two daughters have received their gifts from mum's new make-believe cousin, it's time for bed. Although Trevor and Diane have shared smiles throughout the evening, they both know there's more talking to be done in order to save their weltering marriage. However, after her time online today and placing her daughter's orders, Diane has a plan of her own, but only wants to deliver it once they've gone upstairs to bed.

Ten minutes later a somewhat despondent Trevor gets ready for bed, reluctant to speak so he doesn't have to spend another night on the floor. Looking a little bit sorry for himself, he gets undressed and tucks himself into bed, as Diane walks over to the wardrobe.

"I got something for you today" she beams, hoping this will make up for last night.

"Oh yeah, what is it?" he asks forcing a smile, hoping it's not divorce papers or anything.

She pulls out a box from the wardrobe, walks it over to the bed and hands it over.

"I hope you like them" she says.

Trevor opens the box, not knowing what to expect, then to his surprise finds a new pair of REALLY expensive trainers. He loves them, instantly he wants to put them on, but alarm bells start ringing in his ears...

"What is it? Don't you like them?" she asks, holding her smile, yet looking worried.

"I love them, but where is all this money coming from?" he asks, explaining this morning she informed him there was nothing left of her winnings.

Knowing now that there is just one FINAL little lie to tell, Diane tells her husband about her long-lost cousin and how she gets all this stuff for free. Having no reason to doubt his wife, Trevor swallows it quicker than he did his dinner and thanks her for the lovely gift.

"I know we haven't got any money, but anything you can buy online, you can have and I will order" she explains, making his smile even wider. With no sign of sex, arguments or spatulas tonight, Diane hands her husband the laptop and tells him to surf online stores and make a list of anything he desires.

"What, as in anything, golf clubs and all?" he asks.

"Anything at all" she responds, beaming out a real smile for the first time in ages, seeing him smile for the first time in months.

"Even say, a new six berth tent? How about a new a fish pond for the garden?" he asks.

"If you can buy it online, you can have it" she tells him.

As if he didn't need any more encouragement to REALLY shop for the first in his life, he then confuses her by pushing the laptop away and picking his new trainers off the bed.

"What are you doing? Where are you going?" she asks.

"Just putting my new trainers back in the wardrobe, before I go shopping" he laughs to himself, as the door opens and her face turns to one of thunder.

"Er, yeah, this cousin of yours... Is she responsible for all of this too?" he asks, looking down at the bottom of the wardrobe to find boxes and boxes of shoes.

Diane just stands there, wondering where this line of questioning is going before answering.

"Four hundred pounds, one hundred and twenty-six, eighty-seven" he reads out on each box.

"I know you said your long-lost cousin got all this stuff free, but come on" he adds, not really getting suspicious, but sensing something isn't right.

He slowly walks towards his wife next to the bed "This isn't stolen stuff, is it?" he asks.

"No, I told you, my cousin gets it for free" she answers.

"And there's no sugar-daddy affair going on, or rich millionaire going to declare his love for you and steal you away from me?" he asks. This time she just shakes her head with a tiny smile.

"Then I just have one more question for you" he says.

"One that I don't want, expect or need you to lie about" he adds.

As Diane's stomach falls through the floor and feels her knees start to tremble, Trevor delays asking the final question, or that's how it seems to her...

"If you've got all these shoes for free" he says.

"Could I have more than one pair of trainers for the first time in my life?" he asks with a laugh, huge cowboy dance across the room and a jazzy-hands finish, before sitting himself back down in front of the laptop.

"You just make the list Honey" she tells him.

# CHAPTER 7
## SIMON

It's seven in the evening, a week later in the Luck family household and the place has completely transformed. The Luck's have been spending money like water and who can blame them, seeing as it almost comes as easy as water?

"Who would like a coffee from my new coffee percolator with their dinner?" asks smug looking Trevor dancing across the kitchen floor; still doing the same cowboy dance he started a week ago.

"No to coffee? Maybe a fancy cappuccino then? Or can I tempt any of you with a milky latte?" he adds, singing as he goes.

As Diane has her fancy new cooker which almost cooks and dishes up the meal itself, everyone for the first time looks really happy. Mum has her brand new chrome kitchen, fitted with all the latest gadgets and technology... Dad has new golf clubs, fishing equipment, a fifty inch TV and of course his new percolator... Seventeen year old Hillary opted for nothing but a new wardrobe, as Gucci became her latest label... And fifteen year old Teagan, who turns sixteen tomorrow, is simply happy with a few clothes and her new phone she now lives on.

"So does anyone want anything ordered tomorrow? Because I am planning to shop, shop, shop" sings Diane, sitting down at the table with her family, serving dinner and singling out Teagan because it's her special day.

For the family that always needed and wanted things only a week ago, none of them can think of anything they want to add to the list.

"Trevor, nothing? You don't need anything else from my cousin?" she asks, hoping someone will add something to her empty notepad.

"Nope... Got everything I need right now, thanks Honey" he sings, tucking into his meal.

"Why, what's on your list then?" he asks, unable to imagine there's a new pair of shoes that she hasn't already got.

As the family start to eat, Diane reveals it's always been a dream of hers to have a huge, king-size, four poster bed.

"Ooh, ooh, I would love a new bed too mum" sings Hillary, instantly getting excited by the idea.

"Maybe a circle one that spins round" she adds, claiming she's seen one in a film.

"Yeah me too, but make mine a birthday water bed" sings Teagan, also wanting a piece of the action now.

"Consider it done girls" responds mum, really pleased she's not the only one in the house that still wants more.

As Diane beams from ear to ear and her daughters get excited by their new beds turning up tomorrow, strangely it's Trevor the one with concern written on his smiling face and although excited about the things he's got himself, he still can't quite get his head around it all.

"So, you're going to ask your cousin for three really expensive new beds tomorrow and you don't think she'll mind?" he asks Diane.

"No, why would she? She told me to have whatever I like" answers Diane, as though she's now convinced herself that this cousin really exists.

"And all this stuff we're filling our house with is definitely not stolen?" he asks, showing his true sceptical side.

"It's not stolen, it's all above board and completely legal" she answers, with a smile that believes her own bullshit now too, as Trevor smiles along but knows something doesn't feel right.


A few hours later in the matrimonial bedroom, things for Trevor start to get even more weird, when out of the blue, whilst getting ready for bed, Diane not only initiates sex but talks about it too.

"Shall we, you know... Break our bed for the last time, before we have to break in our new one tomorrow?" she asks, walking seductively across the room towards him.

"Did you by any chance drink the wine before you put it in the sauce for dinner tonight?" he asks, loving her strut, yet feeling slightly uncomfortable about it too.

"No, I didn't touch a drop" she whispers in a sexy deep tone, as she reaches him.

"The only sauce I want tonight is a creamy white one, that comes from your... Coooccckkkk" she adds in the same tone, biting on his ear, as she whispers and lingers onto her last word.

As if Trevor has never experienced his wife like this before, simply because he hasn't, he freaks out a little and backs off dramatically, tripping over invisible things that aren't really on the floor.

"What... What's got into you? What? How?" he stutters, telling her he's not liking what she's doing at all.

Just then seduction goes, sexy goes and Diane returns to normal, as though the make-believe Marvin Gaye music in the background has instantly stopped !!

"Well bloody hell Trevor... Talk about kill the moment" she huffs at him, sounding quite pissed off.

"Kill the moment?" he laughs nervously.

"I thought you might want to kill me with all that biting like a vampire shit" he utters, trying to catch his nervous breath.

"I WAS TRYING TO BE SEXY !!" she growls, taking offence.

"And what's wrong with just asking for sex? Or better still, just doing it?" he snaps back.

As he looks at his pillow on the bed and realises he might be facing a night on the floor again, he quickly changes his tune and asks what this is all about.

"I don't want much in the bedroom Diane... Just sex two or three times a week, that's all" he explains.

"None of this seductive talking, faking it up stuff really bothers me anyway" he continues to say, before asking why the sudden change.

As Trevor successfully defuses what could have been a serious bomb go off in his bedroom, a more calmer Diane sits down on the edge of the bed and starts to explain that she wants change.

"Having this magical notepad... Er, I mean cousin with all this stuff, has made me realise I don't want to be a boring prude any more" she explains.

"You're not a P..."

"I don't want a husband that lies to me either !!" she snaps, before he can finish his sentence.

"Okay..." he whimpers in response, lowering his head.

"I just want to feel alive again... Sexy... Young, you know, do all the things I used to do" she continues to explain.

"There once was a time when I mentioned the word wet and I would only ever be talking about my knickers" she adds.

"MM-mm, yeah, I remember those days" he childishly giggles, tempting to get excited, as she gives him a frown and he stops instantly.

"Now there's more chance of me saying the word if the towels aren't dry in the bathroom or it's raining again outside" she says, making her point.

With support and understanding on her side, Trevor takes her by the hand, stands her up and tells her to change then.

"Yeah but what if I become say, more slutty... What are our daughters going to think of me?" she asks, fearing this most of all.

"Honestly?" he questions.

"I'd say they couldn't blame you for becoming their role model, when they've already achieved it themselves" he answers.

As he laughs to himself, she playfully slaps him across the arm and giggles about it too.

"And what about you darling husband? How are you going to feel about a wife in short skirts and cleavage on show?" she asks.

Without another word to show his full support, he instead shows her his full attention by pressing himself up against her.

"Oh, I see..." she flirts back, as he wraps his arms around her body.

"Let's say we kick this new sexual you into gear straight away, shall we?" he chirps, finally ready for some action from his new wife.

With no money whatsoever to burn, yet shopping done her secret way and a new sexual change about to take place, Diane full of confidence for the first time, pushes her husband down onto the bed and races across the room.

"What are you doing now?" he asks, sitting up on the bed, watching her dive towards the bottom of the wardrobe.

"Hey, you aren't going to put high-heels on are you? Because believe it or not, I ain't really into any of that stepping on my balls with them on stuff" he explains.

Diane listens to what he's got to say, then turns to face him.

"What have you been watching?" she asks screwing up her face, before admitting she's been ordering some other stuff online too, then continues to search behind her shoe boxes.

"And it's not whips and chains, is it? Because I don't want to be taking up any of that freaky bumage either" he says, trying his hardest to see over her shoulder from the bed.

"It's Bondage Sweetie, not bumage and no it's not whips and chains" she responds.

"It's toys !!" she announces, finally finding her secret, secret, secret box.

As he gasps in shock and a little relief, he watches his wife pull out a light blue Rampant Rabbit vibrator and instantly smiles.

"Okay, I'm liking this idea" he chirps with a huge smile, then a gulp, as she takes out the next toy that looks like a long intimidating snake.

"Okay, I understand what it does, but surely you need two women for that?" he questions, knowing his double ended dildo from the next perfectly well.

"Once again Sweetie, that just tells me what kind of porn you actually sit around watching on your own, doesn't it?" she responds, still rummaging through the box, assuring him it works on one person just as well as two lesbians.

"Oh yeah sure, I knew that" he responds, trying to sound all manly.

"But then to me, that's just a waste of a perfectly good end of a bell-end at the end of the thing" he adds, knowing he's educated and right enough to be smug, yet getting his tongue-tied nevertheless.

"Not if I put one end in my vagina and the other end up my bum, it's not" she calmly corrects him, shocks him and almost blows his cock off, hearing things his wife hasn't used or said in a hundred or so years.

Unable to contain himself or wait for the next thing to emerge from the wardrobe, he leaps off the bed to get a better look, as she pulls the next item out...

"And this one baby, well this is the Fist" she tells him, showing him an arm length sex toy, with a clenched fist at the end of it.

"Holy Mother of all... Arms??" he utters, not knowing where to look, as she carries on.

"This is for you... It's a vagina you can stick your thingy inside" she says, pulling out another toy...

"And here's my favourite... The sixteen inch black dildo" she announces, pulling out the final toy, that is in-fact bigger than his arm.
As she picks up and cradles all her new toys ready to be used, Trevor just can't believe what he's witnessing.

"So shall we jump in bed and have some fun?" she sings, heading there herself anyway.

"Yeah, either that or fuck ourselves to death" he mumbles under his breath, unable to keep up with this rapid change his wife is making.
As Diane lays out her toys on the bed and starts to undress, Trevor desperately tries to keep up with her, but she blows him away again by having yet another idea...

"Why don't we use these toys and just for one night, fantasise about someone else?" she suggests.

"Er... A... Can... Er" he stutters, feeling like his penis has already been blown off, now his ears are about to bleed too.

"Come on Sweetie, just for one night" she encourages him.

"You can pretend to be having sex with that celebrity Kylie you like so much" she adds, putting the idea in his head, yet letting his trousers answer for him straight away with a huge smile.
With his smile confirming he's up for it, Diane races across the room in her underwear, smacks her hand against the light switch, making the room completely dark, then hops back on the bed. Although Trevor is trying his hardest to keep up with his wife, he's only just got his pants off, when she lobs the plastic vagina at him, tells him to enjoy Kylie, then picks up her sixteen inches and immediately gets started...

"Hold on a minute" he says, trying to make out his wife in the darkness.

"If I am doing Kylie with this thing, who are you doing with that thing?" he asks, picking up his first sex toy ever.

"MM-mm, wouldn't you like to know?" she moans, confessing it's already slipping in and out of her as they speak.

"Er, well yeah, that's why I asked" he responds, trying to feel around

66

on his toy, as in which is the bottom side and which is the vagina, like it matters.

As he takes up position on the bed and expects the plastic female genitalia to do all the work from above, he waits for groaning Diane to answer his question, but she doesn't.

"Come on... If I am fucking Kylie here, who are you having sex with?" he asks, unwilling to start until she confesses all, then takes a guess himself...

"It's that George guy from the coffee advert isn't it?" he asks.

"MM-mm, no" she answers.

"Okay, okay... How about that black guy with the tiny ears?" he guesses next.

"MM-mm no, but thanks for the idea. Maybe I will have him MM-mm... Sneak in and double team me in a minute" she moans and groans. Knowing he hasn't got started yet or isn't happy to start until she confesses, he decides to stop guessing and ask again...

"MM-mm, yeah, oh yeah... Your dick is so big" she groans.

"WHO'S FUCKING DICK?" he almost yells, wanting in on the action.

"Simon's big dick... MM-mm Simon's" she finally admits, starting to really go for it.

"What, that Simon the presenter from TV?" he asks, whilst holding onto what he feels is the vagina end of his sexual partner tonight.

"Oh no, not up my bum... MM-mm, go on then, just once" she groans, before admitting it's not the guy he's thinking about.

"THEN WHO'S DICK ARE YOU FUCKING?" he really does yell this time, getting slightly frustrated of a sexual kind.

"I told y...ou Simon... MM'mm, Si...mon, it's so har...ard" she mumbles, shuddering whilst answering.

"WHO THE FUCK IS SIMON? SIMON WHO?" he growls, planning himself to fuck Kylie to death in the next few seconds, if she doesn't answer him.

Just then she stops, sits up and grumps at him...

"I don't know his surname... Why are you spoiling this for me?" she growls at him.

"It's just some Simon that works down at the supermarket" she adds, hoping she's answered all of his questions, then asking quite abruptly if she can carry on now, then doing it anyway.

"Oh, that Simon" he sighs, not having a foggy about who he is really, then hearing her get started again with all wet squidgy noises.

Instead of rattling his new wife again so soon or wanting to cause any more of a fuss, he relaxes on his side of the bed and tries to attach his sex toy to himself in the dark. As she groans and moans in pleasure beside him, he starts groaning in discomfort, as his toy just doesn't seem to fit...

"Look, I am sorry to bother you again, but is there a certain way I, you know, have sex with this thing? Because I don't know what I am doing" he asks.

With a huge tut and an aggressive shuffle, she stops for the second time and tries to see what he's doing with it in the dark.

"Well for starters Sweetie, you are supposed to have sex with it, not IT have sex with you" she sighs, working out that he's trying to make the piece of plastic do the cowgirl for him.

"Er?" he shrieks in confusion.

"Put it down on the bed, get on top and hump it" she abruptly tells him, wanting to get on with her huge toy conveniently called Simon now.

"But, I... I just don't get it" he stutters in the dark.

"Get what TREVOR? It's a sex toy, so use it" she grunts, sounding more and more pissed off by the second.

"Well, aren't these things designed to pleasure you and not you pleasure it?" he asks.

"I mean, if I am going to do all the work, I might as well just have sex with you" he adds, making a valid enough point.

"FINE !!" she grunts, slamming her own toy to the floor, then throwing herself back in a strop, waiting for him to get on top.

"Ah now see, that's the sex I am used to" he responds sarcastically, realising exactly what she is doing.

As he sits there refusing to have the same old sex with the same old wife, yet not saying those words exactly, she waits for him to mount her, getting more and more turned off by the second.

"WELL !!" she grunts.

"Are we having sex or not?" she asks, so unromantically, it's scary.

With that and the thought of getting no thanks for his efforts, Trevor simply tells her to go back to her toy Simon and he will try his Kylie thing again.

"Well, only if you insist Sweetie" she chirps, already picking Simon back off the floor.

Knowing he's got no intention of sticking his dick inside a lazy, wife-like piece of plastic, Trevor knows he's got to fake it up and hope his real wife gets a shift on with hers. Although their sex life before wasn't exactly going places, he dreads to think what this new sex life involves, as he wriggles himself into position on the bed.

"MM-mm Simon, you're so... MM-mm, wow, big" she groans, back in her own world of pleasure.

"MM-mm Kylie, you feel so, er?... Rubbery real" he moans, as he fake humps his piece of plastic and tries to compete against his wife's noises...

"OH... So big, so BIG, soo...OOOooo big" she starts to scream.

"Oh Kylie, so... tight, so moist... oh, oh KYLIE, KYLIE, KYLIE" he calls out, wanting to outdo her or at least drown her out.

"Fuck me Simon, fuck me harder... You're so big, so hard, so throbbing inside me" she screams, ready for her oncoming orgasm.

"Oh Kylie, you're so sexily petite... So er?... Tiny... So... So??.... So much better than my wife" he calls out, just clutching at words now.

With that mistake made, his biggest of the night, not only does Diane stop, but wrenches his Kylie toy out from underneath him, still not actually used and tosses it across the room.

"HOW DARE YOU !!" she growls, switching the light on.

"How dare you claim she's better than me" she growls again, watching him sit up in bed, looking as guilty as hell, yet not knowing what for.

"But I wasn't... I wasn't even having sex..."

"OH NO, you're not getting away with it" she snaps.

"So you think Kylie is better than me, do you? Well how about you spend the rest of the night downstairs with her then?" she adds, showing him she's a little bit upset.

"But..."

"But nothing Trevor, I heard you say it" she grunts.

"Now take the new love of your life and go" she barks.

"New love? But you bought it..."

"I SAID GO !!" she screams.

"Never would I make you feel second best to a toy" she ironically explains, picking huge Simon off the floor, telling him to leave again and giving the instinct impression she's going to carry on.

"Second best?" he responds, being forced out of the bed, ready to fight his corner.

"And there's silly me thinking you're fantasising, not actually fucking a real person, with his realistic dick, almost treble the size of mine" he snaps, taking the said toy out of her hand and wriggling it around in front of him.

"You give me that back" she threatens.

"No !!" he answers, still wriggling it around.

"If I don't get to screw Kylie, you don't get to fuck this thing" he adds, putting on his pants, clutching Simon and heading for the door.

"I SAID, GIVE IT BACK !!" she growls.

"No, no, no, no NO !!" he snaps, mocking her clear sexual frustration, as he leaves the bedroom, closing the door behind him.

"YEAH WELL, IT'S NOT A REAL LIFE PERSON, IT'S A TOY AND FOR YOUR INFORMATION, IT'S FOUR TIMES BIGGER THAN YOURS" she screams from inside the room.

Feeling the need to look down at his, Trevor tries to work out if his wife is delivering an insult or an actual fact, then looks up in horror as Hillary stands right in front of him aghast in shock...

"OH... MY... GOD... DAD" she stutters, looking at the huge toy, being flapped around.

"Yeah, I should have guessed you'd be out here" he sighs, looks at his daughter, then casually entering the bedroom again.

Instead of fuelling the flames in the matrimonial bed, he slowly walks over to Diane still sitting there with her arms folded and sits down with her. He gently explains that he thinks there's been a misunderstanding somewhere and wants to correct it, before it blows up in their faces. Feeling the same deep down, Diane agrees without actually agreeing and listens to what he's got to say. He explains that he understands the change she wants to make, but assures she doesn't have to change that much. He also explains that although what she was doing in the dark was okay by him, he's not into plastic himself that much. Finally he tells her that sex toys aren't a threat to him, as long as they use them together.

"Do you get what I am saying Honey?" he asks.

"Don't change too much, want to use them together, not really your thing... Yeah, got it" she replies, fully understanding.

With that Trevor hands over the big toy, slides back into bed and suggests they do it properly this time. As the couple try to reignite the flames, Diane lowers Simon into position. With a smile on Trevor's face, realising it should be fine now; Diane sets to work...

"WHAT THE FUCK ARE YOU DOING?" he then yelps, jumping so high off the bed that he nearly hits the ceiling.

"You said together, play with them together, so I'm going to use it on you first" she confusingly explains, also explaining what his sudden jump was for.

Once Trevor is off the ceiling, counting his lucky stars and assuring her that huge thing doesn't belong in his back passage, he explains that he wants to watch her use it.

"Oh, together as in I use it and you watch?" she sighs, fully understanding now.

With a worried looking smile on his face, Diane attempts it for the second time and runs Simon under the covers and between her own legs this time.

"MM-mm yeah, that's it, you go for it" groans Trevor, finally himself ready to get into some sex toy antics.

## 30 SECONDS LATER...

"You know, this isn't actually working for me" he declares, watching the top of the sheets not do anything much really.

"I'm doing what you asked, I am having sex with it" she responds, having a non-moaning, non-groaning conversation with him.

"Yeah but I can't see anything can I?" he explains, suggesting that if she takes the sheets away, maybe it will spark his interest.

"Fine, but can we have the lights off then?" she asks.

"Er? Again, I don't think I will see much in the dark either" he responds, as though it's not one of the hardest things to work out.

"What, you mean, you want to see it going in and out, like with the lights on?" she asks, as though it IS the hardest thing to work out and sounding slightly horrified about the whole suggestion.

"Oh no, I don't just want to see you fuck it... I want to hear all those noises from before and see you go for it in a major way" he explains, licking his excited lips at the prospect.

"Yeah, I don't mean to burst your perverted bubble Dear, but isn't that a bit creepy?" she asks.

"What, you doing in the light, what you were just doing in the dark?" he asks.

"Yeah, REALLY creepy?" he mocks her.

Realising exactly what he's demanding of her now and threatening to return to the prude she was only this afternoon, Diane refuses to do it in front of him, claiming she can't.

"What do you mean you can't? What's the point of all these sex toys then?" he asks, tempting to get confused himself now.

She explains that him watching her have sex with something else would just feel strange and if honest, a little off putting and wrong.

"Wrong? Don't you think you should have thought about that before buying the things then?" he huffs, realising like every conversation, this one isn't going anywhere either.

"Well yeah I would have, if I knew you'd want to bloody watch me" she responds, closing down on any chance of them having fun.

Not willing to sleep downstairs, not willing to give up on his masturbating yet not masturbating wife, he simply smiles and tells her to forget the toys altogether.

"So what do we do then? Go back to having boring sex?" she asks.

"It's either boring sex or you spice it up without being a bloody P..."

Before he can finish the word, he quickly retracts it and suggests they try something else...

"Oh yeah, like what then?" she asks, clearly a little pissed off with the P word nearly coming out, yet willing to try.

As he sits there thinking about what else they can do, he looks over at the wardrobe and bang, he has an idea...

"You've got loads of new shoes and new clothes, so go and dress up and look all sexy for me" he suggests.

Willing to try anything to correct this night of confusion, Diane accepts the request and within seconds is out of the bed, pulling outfits from the cupboard.

"Okay, you want sexy, I will give you sexy" she declares, with an armful of clothing.

## ONE HOUR, SIXTEEN MINUTES AND TWENTY-TWO SECONDS LATER...

Diane walks back into the bedroom looking a million dollars. She fashions a silky red dress, red shiny shoes and a glowing smile to turn her man on, but...

**HE'S FALLEN ASLEEP !!**

"Well that's charming, that is" she huffs, walking over to the bed.

"CHARMING !!" she shouts, kicking the side of the bed with force.

"What? Where? Who said Simon can stick it in there?" he grumbles in a panic, waking up.

Once he realises Simon isn't in the room or a real person, although he is a real person down at the supermarket, he quickly apologises to his wife and tells her she looks stunning.

"Wow and look at that necklace" he says, pulling her down onto the bed.

"If I didn't know about your cousin, I'd definitely think you were having an affair with a rich guy" he adds, admiring her neck and the necklace.

"MM-mm, just imagine if I was" she responds, instantly getting horny again and returning to fantasy world.

"Do you want to show me what you'd do to me, if I was having an affair?" she asks.

With that Trevor grabs her passionately, forces her down and starts to ravish her...

"Oh, oh, oh, watch you don't rip my dress" she groans, claiming it was really expensive, although it cost her nothing.

"And watch my shoes, I don't want the heel falling off" she adds, making him passionately stop everything he's doing to her.

Just then, whilst on top of her, he does stop...

"This is a fantasy right? I mean, you aren't trying to tell me you're having an affair, are you?" he asks.

"No, of course I ain't silly" she answers, before demanding he don't tug her twenty-nine pound French knickers down too roughly.

"Oh well in that case, I'd better take this necklace off for you too" he says, realising himself that it's the most expensive thing on her body and she's already mentioned everything else.

**JUST THEN**, the magic, the passionate and the eagerness to have sex all disappears for him... He stops in complete shock, slowly backs away and gets off the bed.

"What is it now? What's wrong?" she asks, looking concerned.

"What's that on your neck?" he asks, looking like a pineapple has been inserted into his anus.

"My new necklace?" she guesses.

"And who the bloody hell bought it for you?" he asks.

"Er, my cousin gave it to me?" she guesses again.

"So what's that mark underneath the necklace then?" he asks.

"What mark?" she responds, finally not having an answer.

As poor old confused Trevor starts to assume there is another man involved and the love-bite confirms it, she walks over to the mirror to have a look.

"Oh that... That's where I caught my neck in the clasp whilst putting it on" she explains, but Trevor is no longer with her, as bad thoughts whiz around his head...

"That explains where all the money is really coming from... That explains why we never have sex anymore and that explains the CLEAR bite on your neck" he rattles off, getting himself into a right heartbroken state.

Diane does all she can to convince him he's wrong, but he just won't listen... She confirms the money thing is her cousin, although it's not really and assures him there's no other man, although the delivery guy was on their bed the other day.

"Oh yeah, then why did I smell another guys aftershave on our sheets the other day then?" he asks ironically, sending a bolt of lightning through her body.

"Oh that was, er... See Tia thought I was faking an, er... I can explain" she stutters, knowing the truth doesn't sound much better right now.

"If there is no other man... If this cousin of yours is real, then call her" he says.

"Okay, sure, I'll call her" confused Diane answers.

"No, I mean, let me talk to her" he says, dropping his biggest bombshell to date.

Suddenly Diane realises that the truth must come out, yet her dry throat won't let her speak.

"So, can I talk to her then?" he asks, fearing the worst with everything now.

Diane simply shakes her head...

"She's not real, is she?" he asks, taking a huge gulp.

Diane shakes her head again...

"And this other guy? Would his name happen to be Simon by any chance?" he asks, offering to cry like a heartbroken baby now.

"No, NO, no... There's no other man and there never will be" she responds.

She explains he's got nothing to worry about, but there is something really important she needs to tell him.

"There's nothing wrong with you, is there?" he panics straight away with concern.

"No" she answers.

"And we aren't going to break-up or anything, are we?" he asks next.

"No" she answers, almost laughing at the insanity of his questions.

She quickly explains that her cousin isn't real and that the money for all the stuff is coming from somewhere else, then before he can start guessing again, assures him it's nothing sinister and nothing criminal...

"And no, I haven't been moonlighting as a prostitute either" she giggles.

She promises if he takes the day off work tomorrow, she will tell him everything once the girls have left the house.

"And it's definitely not going to hurt, worry or concern me?" he asks smiling, yet still clearly worried.

"Nothing to worry about at all" she promises.

# CHAPTER 8
# MILKSHAKE

It's yet another normal morning in the Luck family household, that's normal if everyday was different, confusing and full of ups and downs all the time. As Trevor nervously gets ready for his day off work and his wife's explanation, he tries to focus on choosing a breakfast this morning, as Diane stands at the bottom of the stairs.

"Teagan, Hillary, times getting on. Let's get a wriggle on, shall we" she calls out, as the front doorbell rings...

"Oh by the way, Happy Birthday Teagan Sweetie" she adds, whilst answering the door.

"Three beds this morning Mrs Luck" says the delivery guy, addressing her by name now, simply because she's becoming a VERY regular customer.

As Trevor is summoned to help the delivery guy in with the beds and place them in the hallway, Hillary and Teagan come bouncing down the stairs.

"Just one question Honey... Who's putting all these beds upstairs and together?" asks Trevor, puffing.

"Why do you think I asked you to take a day off work Sweetie?" responds Diane, only joking of course, but not funny in the eyes of worried Trevor, who wants answers today.

Once the three beds are crammed into the hallway and the delivery guy has been waved off for yet another day, Teagan asks if her bed is going to be put together first.

"Er, I don't think so Slut-face" huffs Hillary, claiming her round bed will be quicker to put together, doesn't need filling with water and simply because she's the eldest.

"Yeah well, it's my birthday, so I should be first" sixteen year old Teagan boasts, knowing she should by rights get what she wants today.

As if by magic, which is more magic than the magical notepad, mummy Diane confirms this to be a fact, then playfully snaps her fingers and demands Trevor take all three beds up to the bedrooms, starting with Teagan's.

"What on my own?" he moans.

"Oh okay then, I will help you" sighs Diane playfully, lifting Teagan's bed first and getting it ready to carry upstairs.

As the birthday girl leads the way, Diane and Trevor struggle up the stairs with the first big box, which should actually be the lightest, seeing as this mattress should be empty ready to be filled with water once assembled.

Some sweaty five minutes later, the huge box enters Teagan's room, and whilst waiting for it, she's got herself dressed.

"So, what do you think of my sexy school uniform today then?" Teagan asks, spinning on the spot in front of her exhausted parents.

"What school uniform, where?" asks out of breath dad, noticing as usual, she hasn't got much on at all.

"You look beautiful Sweetie, beautiful" boasts Diane, not willing to get into a debate about her choice of outfit this morning.

"Dad?" asks Teagan.

"I want to say... Are you really?... Happy Birthday Teagan" he answers in three different ways, yet at least pleasing his daughter with the final one.

Diane instructs Teagan to get herself off to school, promises her a lovely birthday dinner later, then tussles with the box that won't let anything out, but Teagan wants to see her bed first. Knowing her daughter is going to be late, Diane pulls and pulls at the mattress inside, but it just won't budge...

"Come out you stupid, son-of-a... Barker" she grunts.

"Give a woman a man's job" sighs Trevor, telling her to move out of the way, so he can do it.

Comically, Trevor then takes hold but can't pull the mattress out of the box either, so the married couple team up and tug together.

"Bloody hell, it sounds like the noises that were coming from your room last night" giggles Hillary walking past the door, on the way to her own room.

"Next thing to order... Some sound proofing for the walls" whispers Trevor, refusing to make any more grunting sounds, pulling the mattress even harder.

With one last attempt they both pull as hard as they can and like a rocket the deflated mattress flies out...

"Oh no !!" gasps Diane, as it catches on one of Teagan's drawer handles and it rips right down the middle.

"Nooo-oOOoo !!" screams Teagan, distraught by the tragedy.

"You've ruined it, you've ruined my bed and my perfect birthday" she adds, clearly more distressed by the event than anyone else.

"Calm down Sweetie, I will order you a replacement mattress, don't worry" says the soothing tone of mum's voice.

"No but you don't understand... I was going to... I was..." Teagan bellows out.

"What Sweetie, what were you going to do?" asks Diane, still trying to calm her down.

"She was going to ask a boy over and lose her virginity on her sixteenth birthday tonight" Hillary says, causally walking past the door again, without a care in the world.

"YOU WERE GOING TO WHAT?" growls Trevor, disapproving straight away, then claiming none of that freaky shit will be happening under his roof, sixteen or not.

"No dad, you do enough of that for all of us, don't you?" laughs Hillary, mimicking the size of the dildo he was holding last night, then walking back downstairs, laughing to herself.

As the normal household threatens to meltdown fully and everyone shouts at someone, birthday girl Teagan can't take it anymore, storms down the stairs and out of the house.

"TEAGAN, YOU COME BACK HERE THIS MINUTE" calls Trevor, giving chase.

"Chill out father dear" giggles Hillary, walking past him and out of the front door too.

"I lost my virginity on my fourteenth birthday at home" she confesses.

"YOU DID WHAT? HOW?... GIRLS, DON'T YOU WALK AWAY... Girls, GIRLS how? Girls" calls Trevor, unable to take any more.

"Who cares, I lost mine in the back of a police car when I was thirteen" says Tia, bouncing around the corner, not worrying about the commotion and joining in the fun.

"Tia" groans Trevor, standing in his doorway, saying a disappointed hello.

"Trevor" Tia responds, giving him a filthy flirty eye, then a disappointed look too.

"We were just talking about my daughters not allowed to have sex in this house, I really don't want to hear your slag-bag horror stories" he grunts at her.

"Oh that's okay then" she giggles, asking if Diane's home, then walking inside anyway.

"I had sex in your living room alone... When I stayed over last and in your bed with your friend Paul when you were away on holiday" she confesses, now really feeling included in the commotion.

As Trevor now desperately wishes that he went to work this morning, Tia meets up with Diane in the kitchen, where she is writing the words "water bed mattress" on her notepad.

"Hey Slut bag, what's happening in the Luck residence this morning?" asks Tia, saying hello to her friend, the only way she knows how.

Although Diane is always pleased to see her best friend, this morning she knows Trevor's needs come first, as the poor guy is still waiting patiently for an explanation about last night, whilst he still stands at the front door in shock. Diane tells Tia quickly that she can stay, but she must remain in the kitchen until she and Trevor have had a talk first.

"Oh wow, haven't you done that already?" asks Tia, thinking she understands.

"I know you said he knows about the fling we had, but I assumed you'd have spoken about it by now" she adds, before changing the subject and thanking her for her expensive black dress the other week.

Because Diane didn't really plan on explaining this to Tia this morning

80

and can't really tell her the truth about the magical non-existent cousin, she simply goes along with what Tia is saying and tells her privacy is the key this morning, because this chat is going to be really sensitive.

"No problem babes, I've got your back" sings Tia, buying it straight away.

"If Trevie wants to divorce you because of our fling years ago, we'll get it on again... If he doesn't believe it, we'll show him how lesbians do it ... If he feels left out, then I guess I could be persuaded to have a threesome for his benefit" she adds, ironically suggesting no matter what happens in the other room, they're going to have sex once it's over.

Although Diane is a little gob-smacked by her friends supportive words, she just plays along again and agrees, before demanding Tia stay in the kitchen or masturbates upstairs for all she cares, but just give her the hour she needs. As Trevor steps into the kitchen, Diane spots him and makes a dash towards the door, so he isn't able to hear anything she and Tia are saying. She ushers him into the living room and gives Tia yet another one hour warning sign with her finger.

"Don't you worry Trevie, I ain't a threat to your marriage. Diane is yours, I understand that... But if you don't understand, I'm more than willing to lick her..." Tia calls out, still trying to be supportive, as Diane closes the door, so that confused Trevor can't hear the final bit.

"PUSSY, IN FRONT OF YOU" she shouts, finishing her sentence, as Diane sings a random tune to try and drown her out.

Finally it's here, the moment of truth, the time Diane must confess all, be honest and show her husband some trust.

"So what was all that about then? Was she just calling out what I think she was calling out?" Trevor asks behind the closed living room door, still looking completely confused this morning.

"Oh yeah that... Look don't say anything, but I think Tia is developing a little crush on you and keeps talking about us, you know, having a three way thingy" she responds, ironically already being a little dishonest.

"Eww..." Trevor sounds, instantly screwing up his face.

"Well I am glad you feel that way about my friend Sweetie, but I'm not sure that's the response I actually thought you'd give" she explains.

"Me, you and that thing together in the same bed?" he questions,

81

understanding that she thought he might be up for it.

"I'd rather sleep with the old woman down the pub than put my dick inside Tia's soiled six million times, pants" he explains, making her laugh.

Although the couple stand there making light of the situation, the laughter doesn't last long when they both realise last night's truth needs to be dealt with.

"So come on then, show me what I've taken the day off work for" he says, taking the same long gulp he did last night, then sitting down on the sofa bracing himself...

Diane decides to cut straight to the chase and pulls her magical notepad from her pocket. She explains there's no long lost cousin, because the long lost cousin is in-fact a notepad, which ironically doesn't cut to the chase the way she thought it would and confuses him even more.

"Look, to cut a long story short... If I write something I want down on this notepad, screw it up, then hop, skip and jump, it turns up" she explains, sounding like the craziest woman ever.

"You know what Diane" says Trevor sitting there, listening to the mad but true statement.

"I think I will take that Tia threesome now, if it's okay with you" he adds, claiming it sounds less mental than she does right now.

Realising that words aren't going to do it, she places the laptop down in front of him, loads up an online jewellery store and tells him to pick a watch.

"Don't look at the prices, just pick the one you really like" she demands.

Humouring his wife, Trevor does as he's told and picks a watch costing two thousand pounds.

"Now tell me what the delivery date says" she asks him.

"Between three to five working days" he answers, finding it on the screen, sounding slightly bored with what he thinks is his wife messing about.

Diane writes down the name of the watch, then before feeling completely stupid, she does her little hop... skip... and jump in front of someone for the very first time... Knowing it's coming; she takes a seat next to him on the sofa and gets ready for the oncoming dizzy spell.

"Diane? Diane, are you okay?" she hears him call out, but unable to respond.

"Diane, I think I need to call for help... I think you're having a breakdown of some kind" he adds in a mini panic, in amongst her dizzy haze.

## BANG, SHE'S BACK !!

"Sorry, what were you saying?" she asks.

"My God, are you okay? You're eyes started rolling back in your head and you started to dribble foam out of your mouth" he gasps, sounding really concerned.

She informs him she's completely fine and it's just a simple process she needs to go through to get all this free stuff delivered.

"So you write it down? Do a little dance? Act like a dribbling fruit-cake and these things turn up, do they?" he asks, clearly believing his wife has lost it and may need a straight jacket at any second.

"Let's go and have a cup of coffee, shall we?" she responds assuring him his watch will arrive shortly.

"Yeah, okay, watch... Got it" he responds, trying to work out what to do for the best.

As he follows sane Diane through into the kitchen, wondering whether to call the hospital or Santa himself, Tia meanwhile has taken Diane's words earlier literally and sits at the kitchen table masturbating with one of the new spatulas...

"TIA !!" gasps Diane, noticing her friend sitting there on a stool, jeans down, spatula inserted.

"WHAT? You said I could masturbate, so I am masturbating" Tia responds, not in the least bit shy or embarrassed by two people entering the room.

"FUCK ME !!" gasps Trevor, seeing it for himself.

"MM-mm, get your pants off then" responds Tia, still going.

"Doesn't any female in this house have any sanity left at all? Or is it me? Are you just all normal and I'm the one going crazy?" he asks, startled by Tia brashness, her nakedness and where the spatula is going, as Diane notices him looking.

"Sorry..." he then says to his wife, sorry for looking, yet still bloody looking...

"No it's okay, you watch her Trevor" she answers, shocking poor

Trevor some more, with a statement that would never come out of her mouth.

"If she wants to do that whilst we're in the room, why shouldn't we watch, it's our kitchen?" she explains, knowing she's only got twenty or so minutes to stall her husband, before his special delivery turns up.

The thought of the married couple wanting to watch doesn't put masturbating Tia off and instead kind of turns her on, as she inserts the soiled spatula deeper.

"Do you like what you see Trevie?" she asks, panting at the same time.

As if this wasn't a straight forward enough question, Trevor feeling he's losing it, turns to Diane for the answer.

"Well don't look at me Sweetie... Do you like what you see?" she asks, playing along, before suggesting he must be based on what he was demanding she do herself with her toys last night.

"Er, yeah, kind of" he answers, letting Diane answer for him first, before taking another look at the masturbating slapper on the stool.

"And MM-mm, would you like to show me how, Ooh... How much it's making you throb?" Tia asks, getting into it fully now.

Once again without an answer for Diane's best friend, Trevor simply turns to his wife.

"Again Sweetie, don't look at me... If you feel the need to show her your penis, then show her" Diane says, checking the clock, then working out how long she needs to keep this up for.

As if it's permission granted again, Trevor looks back at Tia's vagina getting more moist by the second and confesses he wouldn't mind showing her.

"MM-mm, show me then" Tia gasps, speeding up her hand, as she groans.

"Show me that BIG... FAT... HARD... MM-mm, throbbing cock" she adds.

With that Trevor shoves his hand down his trousers and starts playing with himself too. Diane although comfortable with this, knows personally she doesn't want it to go any further, so checks the clock again.

"Come on then big boy; show me what you've got... I've heard all the stories from Diane, now I want to see it for myself" Tia groans, starting to get sexually demanding with it too.

For the third time Trevor looks at his wife for permission, yet this time she just smiles and shrugs her shoulders.

"If you want to show her Sweetie, I'm fine with it" she confirms, checking the clock again, but the hands haven't moved very far.

"What's wrong Trevor... Isn't it big enough? Too shy to get it out?" mocks Tia, now taking her sexual behaviour to a whole new level.

As Diane prays that time will pass faster and Tia continues to mock him, Trevor bashes against himself, trying to at least produce a semi.

"Ah, poor old Trevie has stage fright" she mocks some more.

"Well what do you expect?" he grunts, pulling his hand out of his trousers, knowing it's not working.

"I didn't expect to take the day off work, then find myself standing in the kitchen with my wife, her friend masturbating and a demand that I whip my dick out" he adds, claiming he and his penis are in shock.

"Ha, Ha... Trevie can't get it up, Trevie can't get it up" sings Tia, mocking him some more, yet at the same time turning him on enough to actually do it now.

"Right, that does it !!... Want to see it, then here it comes" he responds aggressively, ready to stomp across the kitchen and shut the bitch up.

## DING DONG... DING DONG !!

"Saved by the bell" mutters Diane under her breath, knowing how close that was becoming, then informing Trevor it's for him.

"What, magic notepad and physic powers now, have you?" he responds, tucking his bulge down, giving Tia a frown, then heading for the front door anyway.

"You stay here and do... Do... Oh, just carry on doing whatever it is you're doing" demands Diane, planning to follow Trevor, giving Tia's vagina a strange look, then closing the kitchen door behind her.

Moments later as Trevor answers the door with Diane, he's a little bit stunned to be handed a small parcel by a delivery guy, then even more shocked when the guy addresses his wife as Diane. He's then completely gob-smacked when a huge box comes round the corner and Diane confesses it's Teagan's replacement mattress.

"How? Er... No, how?" he starts to stutter, losing the plot

completely.

"Check the parcel in your hand" says Diane, waving off the delivery guy, then watching her husband open it...

"Oh, it's my new watch" he says casually...

## THUD !!

As Trevor collapses at the front door, Diane catches him and drags his limp body inside. Before bringing him round, she runs into the kitchen and demands masturbating Tia stop what she's doing, go home and come back in a few hours.

"Fine, I've got a rolling pin at home, better than your spatula anyway" she huffs, pulling up her knickers and handing the sticky object to Diane, which isn't received gratefully.

As Diane walks Tia through the hallway and towards the front door, placing the dirty spatula straight in the bin, Trevor starts to come round...

"You're supposed to take a little nap after I've fucked your brains out Trevie, not before it" giggles Tia, stepping over him, then leaving the house.

Diane waves her friend off, Tia claims she'll be back in exactly one hour, fifty-eight minutes and Trevor tries to find his feet.

"Where's she going?" he asks sounding all groggy, unable to focus on the box still in his hand.

Diane informs him she sent her friend home, because they wouldn't be able to discuss what's just happened if she didn't.

"What you mean, Tia doesn't know?" bewildered Trevor asks, finally standing up.

His wife just stands there, shaking her head with a smile on her face.

"Tia that knows everything about everything, doesn't know something?" he asks, desperately needing to hear it again.

"She knows about my make-believe cousin, but not about the notepad" explains Diane.

**THUD !!**, TREVOR HITS THE DECK FOR THE SECOND TIME...

"Oh not again" mumbles Diane.

"I didn't even pass out twice" she sighs, trying to make him comfortable.

As Trevor opens his eyes seconds later, it's not the magical notepad that's bothering him so much, but the magnitude of keeping something from Tia that well.

"I just can't believe Tia doesn't know" he grumbles, choosing not to stand, but to shuffle a little bit, then sit up against the front door.

"How is it possible to keep anything from her?" he asks, as though this is the real magic trick, not the notepad.

Although Diane knows that the make-believe cousin idea fooled everyone, Trevor just can't believe that Tia wouldn't actually know anything, then furthers his dazed questioning by asking how long Diane has been doing this for.

"Oh, er... Only about two weeks" she responds.

"Oh, only two..."

## THUD !!

For the third time in less than five minutes, Trevor loses consciousness again. As Diane concerned for her husband tries to assure herself that passing-out three times doesn't affect your health in anyway, she once again makes him comfortable. Trevor is only out of it for a few seconds and once he comes round, he leaps off the floor, claiming that's enough...

"Okay, no more passing-out, but just let me get this right" he says, dancing on the spot, simply trying to prevent it happening again.

"You've got a magic notepad, I get that... Tia doesn't know anything about it, hard to swallow, but I get that too... But really, two weeks? You've been doing this for two weeks?" he asks, unable to believe her last piece of information.

She looks him in the eye, worried that if she answers he might hit the floor again, so delays answering, with a blank expression on her face.

"Well Diane, have you really been able to do this for a full two weeks?" he asks.

"Sorry yeah, I really didn't want you to faint again" she responds.

"I ain't going to faint because you tell me you have, am I?" he answers.

"But... But you just did a second ago" she stutters, getting a little bit confused herself.

"I didn't faint because you've been doing it for two weeks, I passed-out because you've been doing it for two weeks" he answers.

"Eh?..." she responds, screwing up her face.

"Let's just say if I had this gift, our cupboards wouldn't be full of spatulas and toilet rolls" he explains, asking where's the new car or speedboat.

Finally understanding why he passed-out for the third time, she explains that she just wanted to be careful, find out if she'd get caught first and didn't want anyone getting over excited about it too soon.

"But it is real, isn't it?" he responds.

"I mean, we could go on the internet now and say, book a cruise or even buy a house, couldn't we?" he asks.

"Yeah, I guess we could" she answers, strangely enough not thinking this big herself until now.

## EXACTLY HALF AN HOUR LATER, DING DONG, DING DONG !!

As the married couple run towards the front door and open it, there stands a guy with a set of car keys and simply hands them over with some paperwork.

"You guy's enjoy your new car" say the man, before disappearing into another car waiting to pick him up.

"Better than your toilet rolls and spatulas, isn't it?" says Trevor, standing there mesmerised by the new car sitting in the driveway.

Diane stands there looking at the new red BMW and still can't believe after all this time, that she only thought about buying things at the supermarket.

"Come on then, what are you waiting for?" chirps excited Trevor, already opening the car door.

He jumps in, waits for stunned Diane to jump into the passenger side, then wheel spins away down the street...

As Trevor successfully navigates his way through the busy town and Diane tries to guess where he's taking her, neither of them speak, unable to take in the fact they're in a car they never in a lifetime thought they would be able to afford. It's not until Trevor does a quick left, followed by two rapid right turns, she works out where they are going.

"You're taking me to McDonalds, aren't you?" she asks, as though it wasn't obvious, as he pulls into the car park and zooms round the drive-thru.

"Okay Honey, get that magic notepad out and make it work for our order here" he beams, pulling up at the window, then turning to face the cashier.

"I'll have three Big-Mac meals, five large fries and a couple of Chicken sandwiches too" he says to the guy at the window.

"Trev..." whispers Diane, from the passenger seat.

"Oh and stick a couple of large milkshakes in there with two doughnuts too" he chirps, ignoring his wife's whisper, feeling far too excited about eating whatever he wants.

It's not until he's finished his order and turned to his wife, that he notices she's been trying to get his attention, as the cashier starts to punch the order into the register.

"I hope you've got some spare cash on you, because the notepad won't work here" she whispers.

Instantly Trevor starts to panic and rummages through his pockets, already fearing that he hasn't enough for his large, ain't going to eat it all anyway order. He pulls out some coins amounting to three pounds sixty-two and quickly tries to get the attention of the guy behind the window again.

"Sorry, didn't you finish ordering? I thought you were" says the guy.

"Two milkshakes please" says Trevor, making out he's starting his order again.

"Two more milkshakes to add to your current two milkshakes already ordered Sir?" asks the guy.

"No... Just two milkshakes" Trevor answers.

"Yeah, I've already got that Sir... Two milkshakes, three Big-Mac meals, five large fries and two chicken sandwiches" responds the guy, not understanding that Trevor is actually trying to cancel his first order.

"NO..." sighs Trevor.

"Just TWO milkshakes, NO food whatsoever" he adds.

"So, you want two milkshakes, none of the food you already ordered and not the two milkshakes you've only just shouted for?" asks the worker, starting to get a little confused himself.

"Yeah that's right, just two" responds Trevor.

"Not four?" asks the guy.

With that Trevor puts his foot down and wheel spins away from the window...

"Er, Sweetie... You seem to have left our milkshakes behind" gasps Diane, holding on for dear life, as he skids out of the car park.

"Fuck the milkshakes Diane... They would have probably given us Coke anyway" he huffs, skidding into the next car park and pulling over.

"How about that for a piece of getaway driving?" he asks, gloating at his driving skills.

"Yeah..." sighs his wife, finally letting go of the roof.

"I guess we'll have police cars chasing us from miles around now because you placed the wrong order and then took off" she adds, not sounding very impressed.

"Yeah, but just imagine if that was a bank-job... I would have got away, wouldn't I?" he gloats some more.

"You're forgetting one thing though Sweetie" she giggles, as he listens.

"A getaway driver doesn't hand over the cash first, then take off" she explains, claiming he'd only just given the guy the loose change from his pocket, before committing his ever so brave crime.

Realising his driving skills did impress himself, he knows his macho image has just taken a huge blow and he needs to come back fast...

"Come on then, get your knickers off" he demands out of the blue.

"Let's have car sex, right here, right now" he adds, claiming that he doesn't need to be a getaway driver to be all butch and shit.

Diane thinks he's joking at first, so instead just asks if he's going to go back for their milkshakes now.

"Come on, what are you waiting for? We used to do this years ago, let's do it again" he demands, finally showing her he's serious, as he demands again that she get her pants off.

As Diane turns into an instant wreck and looks out of the window at random passers-by in the not so distant distance, she tries telling him not to be silly, but desperately doesn't want to come across prudish either.

"I'm not being silly Diane, let's do it... I want to have car sex" he chirps, tugging at his zip to subtly reveal himself.

"And that's all you're doing is it? Whipping it out?" she strops, watching him unzip his trousers.

"Er, yeah... It is my penis and it's got to come out to do the sex thing" he answers sarcastically, mocking her as he takes his full erection

90

out, demanding she strip for the third time.

"How comes you can just take it out, yet I've got to get naked?" she asks, not impressed as he sits in the driving seat fondling himself.

"Er, because I wouldn't be able to stick it in you, if you don't take your clothes off" he mocks again, unable to work out why she isn't doing it already.

As though he needed telling, Trevor then realises that his wife isn't going to play along, isn't going to do ANYTHING and is wasting the perfectly good erection that he holds in his hand. With a little huff, a disappointed look and a loud sigh, he admits defeat and starts tucking himself away again...

"Hey, hey, hey... What are you doing?" she asks, realising her prudish behaviour is going to cause another disappointment.

"Just because I don't want to take my clothes off out here in public, doesn't mean I can't... You know, lean down and do something else whilst you drive us home" she adds, lowering her head into his lap, putting a shocked smile on his face and going straight for it, as he pulls away.

## SMASH !!

The car hits a lamppost right in front of them and the moment has passed once again, as she almost bites his helmet off.

"AHHHHH..." he screams out in pain.

"Some driver you are... There's only one lamppost in this car park and you can't even avoid it" she barks, claiming he made her bite her lip, as she sits up again to strop.

"BIT YOUR LIP, YOUR LIP? Honey, you've just chewed into my bell-end" he announces, as though it wasn't already obvious enough to the world.

"Well, it's your fault away" she snaps back at him, checking her poor lip in the mirror.

"Who has car sex in the middle of a random car park anyway?" she huffs.

"Not fucking us, that's who" he grumbles, making sure his penis is still alive, then carefully putting it away.

As Trevor gingerly gets out of the car to check the damage with Diane still thoroughly examining her lip in the mirror, Trevor shouts it's just a dented bumper.

"Hey, talking of bumpers... Do you want to get yourself out here and park your sexy BUMper on this bonnet?" he asks, turning it sexual again. Once again as though she needs to, Diane thinks he is joking at first, then quickly realises he's not.

"Come on Trevor, let's go home please" she begs.

"I have a split lip, the car is bashed and I have a headache coming on anyway" she adds, refusing to get out of the car.

"Yeah, I might have guessed... Bloody prude" he utters to himself, thinking there's no way she can hear him.

"What was that?" she calls from inside the car.

"What?" he asks, stunned by her now dog trained ears.

"You just called me the P word didn't you?" she barks at him, getting a little irate again.

"No, no, don't be silly" he nervously laughs, deciding maybe it's better if he drives them home after all.

"OH NO MISTER... YOU STAY THERE" she calls out, leaning over to lock him out.

"You want to play sexy games, then here's what's going to happen then..." she explains, claiming they aren't going home to Teagan's birthday dinner with him feeling sexually frustrated.

Winding down the window she tells him they are going to play a little fantasy game then instructs him to stick his penis through the window. Straight away this reignites his interest and he jumps to it quicker than a bouncing kangaroo.

"MM-mm, just imagine if someone caught us doing this" she starts to whisper, as he sticks his erection through the window.

"Oh yeah, MM-mm, suck it" he demands, getting turned on instantly.

"Oh no, you beg me to put in my mouth first" she demands, teasing him as hard as she can, then telling him to be quick before someone does walk past.

"Please suck my dick... Please suck it.... Pleeaasseeee..." he starts to beg.

"Oh look, there's someone coming" she announces, as though he isn't begging enough yet.

"Please Diane please... Just put it in your mouth" he says, starting to hump the window.

"Really Trevor... There's someone coming over, stop it" she says, still not willing to suck it for him.

"PLEASE SUCK MY FUCKING DICK" he yells.

"Sir, here are the two milkshakes you ordered" says a voice from behind him, as Trevor shits himself, spins around and shows the McDonalds cashier his junk.

# CHAPTER 9
# PREGNANT

Without speaking to one another for the entire drive home, frustrated and humiliated Trevor pulls up outside the house, knowing he's somehow got to find a smile from somewhere before Teagan comes home for her birthday dinner.

"Not even a bloody sorry, not even a bloody sorry" he grumbles under his breath, slamming the car door shut.

"I don't understand what I've got to be sorry for" Diane responds, over hearing the loud enough grumble.

"I told you at least three times that someone was coming" she explains, claiming it wasn't her fault he wanted car sex in the first place and it wasn't her fault he didn't listen.

"Yeah but you fucking told me it was a make-believe fantasy" he erupts, opening the front door.

"Just like your make-believe cousin that isn't real either" he adds, making his valid point and her feel guilty in the process.

With that she does back down and insists as soon as they get inside, she's going to make it up to him BIG TIME !!

Although Trevor is gutted he took the day off work for this outcome, he knows that one simple lightening of the scrotum should make him a less grumpy bastard. With that they both head inside to have non-exhibition sex in the comfort of their home.

"So, where did this new BMW come from?" asks Tia, magically appearing from nowhere, claiming she said she'd be back in an hour, then pushing past both of them at the doorway.

"Er Tia, I think... Tia, we need a little time on our own please" stutters Diane, unable to stop her friend from marching straight into the kitchen.

"Time, slim" sings Tia not listening.

"What could you possibly need more time for, that Trev's thickie-dicky couldn't do in the hour just passed?" she asks, claiming she went home and fucked her rolling pin twice.

"Tia, we haven't had sex yet and were just about to, so if you don't mind" Trevor blurts out abruptly.

"No, I don't mind. I like watching anyway" Tia responds, not giving the answer neither of them wanted.

"Tia, you aren't watching" grunts Diane, realising she doesn't need this right now.

"Why?" Tia responds.

"That's final Tia, not up for discussion... You're not watching" Diane informs her again, trying to take it seriously, as her friend jokes away.

"Why?" Tia responds again.

"TIA !!" snaps Trevor.

"We're going to fuck now... Which means you need to fuck off !!" he snaps, delivering it the tough love way.

"Fine !!" Tia strops.

"But before I go, where did the new car come from?" she asks.

## FIVE MINUTES LATER...

"Go Diane go, ride his cock like a steam train" Tia sings, standing at the end of the marital bed, watching her friends have sex under the sheets.

"Come on Sweetie, make it a quick one" groans Diane at a whisper in his ear, claiming they can do a longer version later.

"Don't you worry, I intend to" he responds, grunting, thrusting and giving his all.

"If we MM-mm, would have told her about the car... MM-mm, she'd want everything" Diane explains quietly during the intercourse, quiet enough not to be heard by singing Tia...

"FASTER TREVIE, FASTER... SOAK HIS COCK DIANE, SOAK IT" she screams out, loving her very own porno, then gets ready to leap on the bed herself and join in.

"Ahhhhhhhh..." Trevor sounds out, as he shoots his load just in time, then falls off his wife instantly.

"No, no, no" sulks singing Tia, claiming that can't be it.

"You've only been going for forty-two seconds... Come on, come on, stop lying... I want to play too" she adds, explaining that's not enough time for a horny woman like her to cum, let alone a can't get it up man.
As Diane sits herself up under the sheets, she explains that it was quick because they taught themselves to do the fast version when they became parents.

"Why?" asks Tia, still sulking.

"So children wouldn't walk in on us doing it" answers Diane.

"And are you sure this fast version is actually worth taking your knickers off for?" asks Tia, screwing up her face, claiming she'd kick a man's arse if she took hers off for that.

"You WERE about to take them off, weren't you Tia?" laughs Trevor, taking the slight revenge piss out of her a little, claiming that means she would have had to kick his backside then.

"No Trevie... I would have simply let you fart and fall asleep, then put right all the missed orgasms Diane never had myself" she playfully snaps back, shutting him up, then suddenly looking at Diane with a flirtatious glint in her eye.

"What?... What are you looking at me like that for?" giggles Diane nervously.

"Now Trevie knows we got it on, now he's just cum, we could, you know..." Tia flirts.

"No, NO, no !!" snaps Diane.

"There's no way I can do that, not here, not with you, no, no, no" she adds, threatening to work herself up into a homophobic tizzy.
Suddenly as if Tia's request wasn't strange enough, Trevor then picks on her too and insists she go for it.

"But, what? But I've just cum, haven't I SWEETIE?" she answers stuttering, before getting a little pissed off with him herself.

"Yeah but that was only a small one... Not a BIG-MAC one" he responds smugly, pointing out how he's about to get revenge on her for the McDonalds thing earlier.

As adamant Diane searches for a way out and Tia sits at the end of the bed licking her lips, Trevor gets himself ready for the show of his life.

"Come on then SWEETIE, let's see this lesbian show" he sings, calling her by the name she often gives to him.

"You wouldn't want me or your friend to think you're Pru... P... Perfectly straight, would you?" he asks, tempting to wind her up with the magical P word she hates so much.

"GO ON, SAY IT" she suddenly snaps, spotting her way out, if she can make him call her it.

"Nope" he smirks, with a big grin on his face.

"You were going to call me it, weren't you?" she forcefully asks, needing his help desperately.

"No sorry, I wasn't going to call you anything" he responds, holding his huge smile.

Just then it's Tia that gets bored, so starts unbuttoning her skirt...

"Come on Diane, we've done it before... It's only in front of your husband, so stop being a fucking prude" she playfully attacks, saying the magic word, yet it coming from the wrong person.

Finally it's Trevor that saves the day, as when Diane realises she's about to go all girl-on-girl again for the first time in years, he explodes into a fake rage...

"Oh I see" he barks.

"It's okay for her to call you a PRUDE, but when I call you a PRUDE, I get a kick in the nuts for it" he adds.

Once Diane realises he's faking it up for her benefit and that she owes him big time for doing so, she plays along too and makes Tia feel uncomfortable about it.

"Look, if you two need to have this out, I will give you some space" Tia nervously says.

"That would be great Tia, great" responds Diane, claiming they've just got to sort out this final issue and that she can come back for Teagan's birthday dinner later tonight.

With that Tia hops off the bed and leaves the room.

"Well that was a close call, wasn't it?" Diane sighs, giggles and lies back on the bed in relief.

"Close call? Close call? It's fucking true... Tia gets away with anything, I don't" he huffs, turning what was a playful plan back on her. As Diane tries to catch up again, Trevor is on his knees and tugging at Diane's pants for real this time.

"I can't believe you were going to fuck another woman right here in front of me" he grunts, getting himself really fired up for the sex they're about to have.

"But we've just done it, you've just cum" she stutters, unable to do the catching up thing, as she tries to keep her legs closed and knickers on.

"I faked it because your friend was watching, now I'm going to do it for real" he answers, showing her he is capable of growing, then aiming his stiff rod towards her vagina.

As he huffs and puffs whilst moving into position, she huffs and puffs to get him off.

"Sweetie please, can't we do this later? I have a really bad headache coming on" she asks him.

"Not a fucking chance" he growls, lying his body weight on top of her.

"Really Sweetie, really... I don't want to do this now" she cries out, insisting he stop.

With that Trevor for the third time sexually frustrated today stops, pulls away and leaps off the bed.

"This is so wrong, SO fucking wrong" he yells, calling her a prude in the process.

"Once Teagan's party is over tonight, I want... I need... I must have some good fucking sex" he adds, done with talking.

"Where are you going now?" she asks sounding concerned, as she watches him open the bedroom door to leave.

"I'm going to fix all these bloody beds, aren't I?" he answers, slamming the door behind him.


Four hours later once the beds are all assembled, the girls have bounced all over them and they've all finished Teagan's birthday dinner, things are calm and happy. Calm and happy, yet underneath simmering like a volcano ready to erupt. Trevor goes around the table one by one and asks the four women in his life if they've had a good evening and what

99

they plan to do now.

"Teagan?" he asks.

"New bed, generous new cousin... Best birthday ever" Teagan sings, beaming from ear to ear.

"And what are you doing now?" asks dad.

"Just going to go to my room to text a few friends" she answers playing with her phone as she speaks, which coincidentally is to the boy she plans to lose her virginity with later tonight.

As dad's suspicious smile declares it knows all, he moves onto Tia, sitting next to his daughter.

"I guess with all that alcohol consumed, you'll want to sleep on the sofa AGAIN?" he asks.

Tipsy Tia doesn't answer, yet smiles, nods her head and gives him a wink.

"And what about you Hillary? You haven't eaten much tonight" he asks, noticing in-fact she hasn't touched any of the food on her plate.

"Yeah sorry dad, just feeling a little sick" she responds, before heaving at the table, then racing out of the room.

"PREGNANT" Diane, Trevor and Tia all guess at once, yet in different ways...

Trevor says it shocked by his guess, then shocked some more the other two thought it too... Diane says it feeling shocked too, yet more startled that Trevor seems to be taking it really well, or the fact she's going to be a prudish grandmother now... Then Tia, well Tia, she just thinks the whole thing is hilarious !!

"Who's pregnant?" asks Teagan, shocked herself that all three just said the same thing at the same time, yet not knowing who actually said it first, so she can jinx the other two.

"And this is why Teagan, no matter what you are thinking, planning or feel you need to do now you're sixteen, there's no rush" Trevor explains pointing out the fact, he hasn't forgotten what they DIDN'T speak about this morning before school.

"Now, now Trevor, we don't know if Hillary is pregnant yet" states Diane, refusing to jump the gun like him, yet kind of doing it seconds ago when she considered her new grandmother role.

Two minutes later, Hillary walks back into the room, looking refreshed and better.

100

"You okay Sweetie?" asks mum, looking a little concerned.

"Yeah, of course I am" Hillary answers.

"So there's nothing wrong? Nothing we need to know?" asks Trevor, feeling his line of questioning is a little better.

"Nope, nothing" answers Hillary, all smiles.

"Are you fucking pregnant, you Slut?" asks Tia, opting for the no bullshit approach.

Instantly Hillary's face drops and she knows she's been busted...

"How? Why? How did you find out?" she stutters, pretty much confirming without saying it, that she is pregnant.

As horrified Diane sits there aghast by the news and Trevor threatens to do his passing-out thing once more, it's Teagan that speaks first and congratulates her seventeen year old sister on her news.

"Er, thanks? I think, I don't know..." stutters Hillary, smiling one second, then looking confused the next.

"Don't know what? If you're keeping it?" asks Tia, finally getting over the shock herself, although she thought it was funny moments ago.

"Of course she ain't keeping it, she's only seventeen years old" snaps Diane, instantly making her mind up for them all.

"Excuse me, but we take our responsibilities in this house seriously thank you... There will be no talk of getting rid of any baby" barks Trevor, as Hillary's head bounces backwards and forwards between her parents like a tennis ball.

With arguments ready to ruin the perfect evening, Tia makes a point of wishing young Teagan a happy birthday again and suggests they all sleep on the matter before making decisions.

"Yeah, that's a good idea Tia" responds Trevor, looking over at his eldest daughter.

"So who's the fucking father, I will kill the little shit" he then asks, strangely deciding he should ask this question before sleeping on it.


Two hours after the shocking news, Trevor and Diane find themselves in their bedroom, unable to talk about anything now. As Trevor gets undressed, then dressed again, then undressed, he doesn't know what to do for the best.

"Are you coming to bed tonight?" asks nightie wearing Diane, sliding underneath the sheets.

Trevor explains that he's about to have a breakdown, then undresses himself for the third time.

"It's okay Sweetie, it's just the shock" she explains, trying to reassure him.

"Shock? Shock?" he laughs hysterically.

"My seventeen year old daughter has just declared she's pregnant... I have a sixteen year old trying to sneak god-knows who into our house tonight for sex" he adds.

"Calm down Sweetie and come to bed" she insists, claiming him getting into a state isn't going to help anyone.

"What to have sex with you Miss Prude, I can't do anything without stopping in the middle?" he growls.

"Well if you come to bed, I won't stop in the middle tonight" she answers, flipping back the sheets to let him in.

"You want sex now? Sex now?" he growls again, in shock.

"What with your magical notepad beside you and your slut of a friend downstairs on my sofa, threatening to walk in and join us at any minute? No thank you very much" he adds, unable to work out why she'd suggest such a thing.

With a "That does it" he gets dressed again and claims no-one under his watch is going to get pregnant tonight.

"What are you doing now?" she asks.

"I'm going to make sure no-one gets into this house tonight and sleeps with one of my daughters" he answers, leaving Diane sitting in bed, the room and his sanity behind.

"DON'T FORGET HORNY TIA IS DOWN THERE ON THE SOFA" Diane calls out from the bedroom, as he does a quick U-turn on the stairs and marches back up again.

Instead of facing man-eating Tia in the living room, he then opts for sitting outside Teagan's bedroom, then thinks of the trouble he will get into if caught, so decides to open the hallway window instead...

"If anyone tries to sneak into my house tonight, I will know about it" he huffs to himself, climbing out onto the roof, ready to do his very own stake-out of his property.

He sits down on the roof with a clear vantage point of his daughters windows and the front door, then realises he's freezing cold.

"It'll be a lot warmer doing this from the front door" he huffs again, climbing back through the window and inside again.


Half an hour later as night falls on the house and everything is silent, Trevor finds himself sitting at the front door, waiting for something to happen. Suddenly there's a noise, a window opening perhaps...

"Not tonight you dirty fucking Scum-bag" he growls feeling this is it, the moment he steps up, becomes a real dad and fends off his daughter's predator.

He sneaks back upstairs, assuming it's Teagan's window that's been opened and finds himself outside her room.

"Okay Scum-bag, got you !!" he calls out, bursting into his daughters room, then shockingly finding her not in there.

As he thinks it's Teagan that's jumped out of the window herself, he decides to walk over and lock it, so she has to face him on her return. Whilst he's doing that, things in the house are moving about quite swiftly. Diane has got up to find out what he was shouting about and has headed downstairs... The living room window has been left open by tipsy Tia, who has climbed out of it and is heading for an upstairs window via the drainpipe... And Teagan is in the bathroom having a wee, although her father thinks she's out... Feeling that there's nothing he can do until absent Teagan returns now, although she's not, he decides to call it a night. Unfortunately, in his own bedroom, Tia has managed to climb through his window and has jumped into the empty bed. As Trevor enters his dark bedroom, Diane makes herself a coffee downstairs and Teagan almost walks past her father on the landing, Tia has started masturbating in the marital bed...

"MM-mm, now that's the wife I've been waiting for" he chirps, seeing the shape of his wife, yet it being the shape of Tia instead, jerking herself off under the sheets.

Trevor slides into bed and instantly presses his erect dong against her body.

"You want to try sucking it like you did earlier, but carry on playing with yourself too?" he asks at a whisper.

As if all his notepad wishes are coming true, lips wrap around his solid stick and begin to go wild on his shaft...

"MM-mm, wow, yeah... My god, I always knew you could do this" he groans, receiving what is his best blow-job to date.

# THUD !!

The bedroom door comes crashing open...

"WHAT THE HELL IS GOING ON IN HERE?" barks Diane switching the light on, as Tia emerges from the sheets, holding Trevor's penis in her hand.

"WHAT THE FUCK !!" he screams, leaping off the bed, springing up faster than his penis did moments ago.

"How? What? Who said? What are you doing here?" he stutters, standing next to his wife at the door, erection on full show, as they both look at Tia naked on their bed.

"Don't tell me Sweetie... You thought she was me? It was dark? You don't know how she got there?" sighs Diane, threatening to say she's heard it all before, yet only ever really hearing it before from films.

"Er?... Yeah, yeah and YES" he answers, still in complete, stand to attention shock.

"Tia?" Diane asks, looking over at her friend on the bed again.

"What? It wasn't me. He told me to suck it" she answers, trying to get rid of her own guilt.

"You said what?" barks Diane, giving Trevor more daggers.

"Yeah, but only because I thought it was you" he responds.

"It's not my fault the best blow-job I have ever..." he adds before stopping himself, realising he's saying too much.

"Ahh, that's lovely Trevor. Am I really the best?" asks Tia, all smiles on the bed.

"Wow, not half" he answers looking over at her, somehow forgetting his wife is standing there too.

"You haven't got such a bad package down there yourself" she responds.

Meanwhile whilst Trevor and Tia's flames threaten to reignite and Diane stands there listening, Teagan has indeed managed to sneak her boyfriend past everyone and they've entered her bedroom.

"When you two have quite finished paying each-other compliments, will you kindly remember, there's a wife and friend standing right here with you" Diane barks.

In a situation none of them know what to do with next and although Tia does suggest a threesome might ease the confusion, the mood has definitely passed for a least one of them.

"So what do we do now?" asks Trevor, standing there and only now feeling the time is right to cover up his private parts with his hand.

"Well you've had my suggestion" gleams Tia, still on the bed.

"I think we should all leave sex for tonight and talk about it again in the morning" says Diane, which is more of a command than a suggestion.

"Says the prude in the room" grunts Trevor under his breath.

With nothing else left to say, Tia gets off the bed, heads for the door and wishes them both a goodnight.

"Tia, just one question" says Trevor.

"Yes Mr Thick-Dick" she responds, turning round flirtatiously, then receiving daggers from Diane.

"How did you get in here?" he asks, still confused about the whole thing.

"Through the window" she chirps.

"See, I knew I heard a window opening somewhere" he chirps in response, like it matters now.

"Hold on, why the window and not the door?" asks Diane, getting confused herself now.

"Er, because I saw it on a porn film a while back" she answers, mocking her friend's dumb question.

"What and they don't walk through doors in those films?" asks Diane.

"Yeah, sure they do" answers Tia.

"But the one I watched with the window, was the only one I've seen that saw a married man fucking his wife's best friend" she announces, subtly but strangely confessing that was her plan in the first place.


In the morning, which for the first time ever isn't a normal morning in the Luck family household, Diane wakes up alone. Instantly after a short groggy spell, she quickly leaps out of bed and fears the worst.

"Please don't be with her, please don't be with her" she panics, racing across the landing, then towards the stairs in her nightie.

"Please don't be sleeping with my man, please Tia" she continues to panic, leaping down the staircase, still very much fearing the worst.

As she reaches the bottom and dives into the living room, Tia and Trevor are sitting there fully clothed, just talking.

"Thank goodness" mumbles a relieved looking Diane.

"You thought we were having sex, didn't you?" asks Tia, putting her friend straight on the spot.

"No..." sings Diane, knowing they both know it's true anyway.

"Yes you did... You thought me and your Trevor got up this morning and fucked each-other silly" Tia sings, claiming her friend shouldn't be so paranoid.

"Well what do you expect? I did catch you giving my husband a BJ last night, after all" explains Diane, before confessing how grateful she is they're not humping each-other.

"That's okay Diane, don't worry about it" answers Tia, still all smiles, as Diane heads for the hallway to shout on the girls.

"He is leaving you for me though" she adds.

"TEAGAN, HILLARY... What the... Sodding hell !!" Diane calls up the stairs before realising what her friend has just said.

"You're joking right? Not funny Tia, not funny at all" giggles Diane, walking back into the room.

Neither of them say a word...

"You are joking... Tell me you're joking... Trevor?" she says, instantly losing her laughter and fearing that worst again.

"Okay I'm off to work, so I will let you girls talk about this" he responds, quickly like he does, making his exit.

Diane watches her husband walk past her, fail to give her a kiss goodbye for the first time in years, then turns to Tia for answers. Suddenly Trevor walks back in, feeling the need to get something off his chest...

"If you weren't such a nag... Weren't such a bore in the bedroom... Didn't moan about not having any money all the time and stopped bitching at our daughters, this wouldn't be happening" he says, attacking her one second, then feeling sorry for her the next.

"And you choose Tia my friend as a replacement? Tia without any money? Tia the biggest bitch on the planet? Tia without any daughters of her own?" growls Diane, not fully understanding.

"Yeah but she's a filthy slut in the bedroom and that's one more

106

thing than you've got" he whispers, ducking in-case something comes flying towards him.

"Tia, is this true? Are you really stealing my husband?" Diane questions, turning back to her friend, looking really upset.

# CHAPTER 10
# NOTEPAD

As a dumbfounded Diane stands waiting for answers, those answers become clear by the other two's silence. In a mad bid to save her flagging marriage and knowing her friend far too well, Diane then decides to tell Tia everything about the magical notepad.

"How about if I offered you anything in the world? Would you then leave my husband alone?" she asks Tia, unable to believe she's having this conversation.

Tia weighs up the offer for a few seconds, giving the impression she can be bought.

"I don't know... Love is a powerful thing Diane" Tia answers, then strangely giving the impression she can't.

"Yeah and it's my love you are stealing" Diane cries out, close to tears.

As Trevor stands there silently watching his wife begin to meltdown, daughters Hillary and Teagan come bouncing down the stairs and into the kitchen.

"Ooh, what's happening here? This looks tense" Hillary mocks playfully.

"Your father has decided he'd rather spend the rest of his life with Tia and not me" answers Diane, getting in the first word, as though anyone else was going to speak anyway.

"Oh..." sighs non-responsive Hillary, reaching for the toaster.

"Oh? Oh? Is that really all you've got to say Hillary?" asks confused mum, expected to get the backing of her eldest at least.

"No, sorry mum, that's not all I've got to say" apologises Hillary.

"Thanks for understanding about the me being pregnant thing last night dad" she adds, kissing her father on the cheek, then casually leaving the house by the back door.

As stunned Diane doesn't understand anything that's going on, she then turns to her youngest and asks if she's got an opinion, whilst she herself pulls up her long socks, ready for another slut fuelled day at school.

"Well..." responds Teagan.

"Tia's a great person and she's funny, so as long as she makes dad happy, I am happy" she chirps.

"TEAGAN !!" snaps horrified Diane, completely blown away.

"Isn't my little baby girl bothered that your father is leaving us?" asks Diane, feeling Teagan can't have heard it correctly.

"I'm not your baby girl any more mum, I lost my virginity last night" the youngest boasts, before leaving the house the same way Hillary did minutes ago.

"Er, ah... I? Wow !!" Diane stutters, feeling the need to take a seat, then nearly missing it as she does.

"Did you hear that Trevor? Our baby girl had sex last night?" she asks, needing a sane conversation from someone this morning, then attacking his crappy lookout skills.

"That's great news Diane, great news" he chirps, not in the slightest bit interested about her concern, as he flirts with Tia.

As Diane holds her head in her hands and believes she's having a nightmare, she then decides to try and pay off Tia one more time...

"How about a house Tia? How about if I bought you a house to leave Trevor alone?" she asks, now sounding desperate.

"A mansion couldn't part me from this stud-muffin, sorry Diane" answers Tia, flirting some more with the husband as she speaks.

"OKAY THEN..." grunts Diane.

"How about a new wardrobe, new designer clothes, perfume and everything material like yourself, you'll ever need?" she asks.

This time she's caught Tia's attention, but she doesn't believe Diane can pull it off.

"Are you telling me your cousin can buy me any house I want, anything I desire and all I've got to do is leave Trevor alone?" Tia asks, as Trevor's face drops through the floor.

"ANYTHING AND AS MUCH AS YOU LIKE" Diane explains, finally making the breakthrough.

As Tia's interest is sparked and Diane races across the room for her notepad, Tia has a plan of her own...

"I will order all this stuff, then once I have it, I will leave with you anyway" she whispers to Trevor, with a huge cunning smile on her face.

Suddenly it's Trevor that feels bad and insists she can't do that...

"It's one thing me leaving her, but another thing taking the piss" he whispers, not happy about the plan at all.

Diane races back across the room and slams down her magical notepad...

"So, do we have a deal Tia?" she asks.

Tia looks at Trevor for the answer, doesn't wait for it, then agrees anyway. A huge house, a massive new wardrobe and three new cars are added to Diane's notepad within seconds.

"So all this in half an hour and you walk away from me and Trevor for good?" asks Diane, needing confirmation before doing her thing.

Tia looks at Trevor for the second time, then simply agrees whether he likes it or not...

"Oh, but one last thing I want placed on that list, before any of the other stuff turns up" says Tia.

"I want another one of those spatulas" she declares.

As confused Diane gives her a strange look, then starts writing it down, Tia turns to Trevor and confesses this is her cunning master plan to get Diane out of the house.

"In five minutes I am going to be all over you like a rash" she whispers, letting the sexual fire transport from her eyes into his.

Soon enough Tia's little plan backfires, when Diane forgets writing it down, then pulls a spare one from the cupboard and hands it over...

"No, no, no... I want a new one from the shop" Tia insists, claiming it's from the shop right now or the deal is off.

Expecting Diane to now leave the house, the wife doesn't question the bizarre request and simply writes it down for real this time.

"So, you'll be off down the supermarket then, will you?" asks Tia.

"Yeah, but I will be back in no time with the rest of your stuff too" sings Diane, tearing off the piece of paper, then heading through into the living room alone, warning horrid Tia to keep her hands to herself whilst she's gone.

"Okay, let's do this Sexy... We've got at least half an hour to fuck ourselves silly" chirps Tia, tugging at Trevor's trousers the minute Diane's back is turned.

"Let me just make sure she's gone first" he responds, backing off slightly, knowing that he's seen Diane do what she's about to do before and that it didn't result in her leaving the house.

Little does Trevor know, that when he does fight off gagging for it Tia, Diane isn't in the living room and has actually left for that supermarket check-out via dizzy airlines.


"Thank you very much, please come again" says the voice of the cashier, Diane knows she's been waiting all of ten seconds to hear.

As she slowly begins to open her eyes though, nothing happened and everything is blank...

"Thank you very much, please come again" says the voice again.

Diane in her dizzy state of mind, blinks hard, blinks again, but nothing but a dull black space of emptiness blocks her vision.

"What's going on? I can hear you, but can't see you" she calls out, knowing something isn't right, as she continues to spin.

## NOTHING !!

"Hello, can anyone hear me?" she calls out again.

## NOTHING, AGAIN !!

As soon as she realises that it hasn't gone to plan and the voice saying the same thing fades into the background, Diane knows she's in trouble. In one final bid to land herself in that supermarket, she calls out for Trevor, but again nothing happens...


It's yet another normal morning in the Luck family household, yet Diane hasn't got up to call the girls from their beds this morning.

"Diane Honey, are you getting up today?" asks Trevor's voice.

She slowly opens her eyes, then feeling groggy, believes it's all been a bad dream.

"Trevor?" she grumbles, in hope she's right.

"Yeah it's me... You've slept in" he informs her, with a loving smile.

"I've got to go to work now, but the last of the milk has been used by our lovely thoughtful daughters" he explains, waiting nervously for her to respond.

"That's fine" she grumbles again, before jumping up and leaping off the bed all excited.

"Don't stress, I will run down to the shop right now if... What? Did you say it's fine?" shocked Trevor asks, unable to believe his ears.

With that he follows her down the stairs and watches her race into the kitchen to wish her daughters a good morning. Hillary dressed in a smart suit, ready for her first day at work gets the first kiss on the cheek from mum.

"Good morning mum, are you okay?" asks Hillary, unable to believe her mother's mood this morning.

Next it's Teagan dressed in her school uniform suitable for church...

"You know Sweetie, I think we can do a lot better than this" Diane chirps, unbuttoning Teagan's blouse a little bit, insisting she needs to become a little sexier.

"Really? But you've always been so P... Really?" gasps Teagan, with a glowing yet confused smile too.

As both daughters love that there mother is not the nag she normally is, Trevor informs her they are also out of his favourite honey cereal.

"Today's the day before our Teagan's big sixteenth birthday, isn't it?" Diane responds, slightly confused by the date, then having it confirmed by the up and coming birthday girl herself.

"So let's concentrate on that today and plan the biggest party EVER" she announces.

As her stunned family watch as she glides around the kitchen, Diane feels she's been given a second chance at life, yet Trevor is concerned...

"You didn't by any chance hit your head getting out of bed this morning, did you?" he asks, looking concerned.

"I mean, no dizzy spells? The room isn't spinning at all? No headaches?" he asks.

"For once in my life, no, the room ISN'T spinning" she sings, walking over to him.

"And as for hitting my head on the head... Well that comes later when you fuck my brains out tonight" she whispers seductively, as he chokes on his final mouthful of coffee.

Although he's NEVER heard his prudish wife talk like this before, he's more than pleased she has done so and stands there speechless. Suddenly the front door opens and in walks a different, more respectable looking Tia in a long knee length grey skirt.

"Oh... My... God" gasps Diane, noticing her best friend, then complimenting her on her womanly fashionable look.

"Ah, fuck you Diane, I knew you'd mock my change in style" responds the same old Tia, hitching up the skirt, quickly tarting herself up, then asking if Diane is feeling okay, because she's being extra jolly this morning.

"Yeah, I am fine Tia, fine" Diane responds.

"What, no money troubles? No issues from school? No nothing to moan about in life?" asks Tia, shocked herself now.

"As long as my beautiful family are happy and we're all together, nothing else matters?" chirps Diane, feeling for the first time in her life, without actually really knowing it, stress free.

"Mum... Since you're in such a good mood... I know there isn't any money, but I've found these boots I really love" says Hillary, chancing what only the other day, would have seen her get a telling off.

"I will see what I can do" chirps Diane, smiling across the room at her although not a magical notepad, but magical to her because it's just changed her life.

## OTHER JIMMY BOOKS

## COMING NEXT

*"Nymph-no, Thank you – Due Summer '2015*

{When twenty-five year old Sara Lowe is left heartbroken after losing yet another decent boyfriend because of her own stupid mistakes, it's just one in a long line of relationships she's pressed the self-destruct button on, because she is far too easily lead. But she's not lead by people or her best friend Nicole, she's lead by her persuasive knickers that don't seem to have the ability to say no to anything. Every time a random guy gives her attention, or even glances in her direction, her knickers are simply unable to stay around her waist. With a rapidly growing reputation of being the local nymphomaniac, Sara is determined to say "Nymph-no thank you". Only question is, how does she do this when she admittedly enjoys sex a great deal and even the likes of Nicole believes it's just part of her personality?}

## www.goodreads.com

Printed in Great Britain
by Amazon.co.uk, Ltd.,
Marston Gate.